# BLACK OAK

# WHEN THE COLD WIND BLOWS

## Charles Grant

A ROC BOOK

ROC
Published by New American Library, a division of
Penguin Putnam Inc., 375 Hudson Street,
New York, New York 10014, U.S.A.
Penguin Books Ltd, 27 Wrights Lane,
London W8 5TZ, England
Penguin Books Australia Ltd,
Ringwood, Victoria, Australia
Penguin Books Canada Ltd, 10 Alcorn Avenue,
Toronto, Ontario, Canada M4V 3B2
Penguin Books (N.Z.) Ltd, 182–190 Wairau Road,
Auckland 10, New Zealand

Penguin Books Ltd, Registered Offices:
Harmondsworth, Middlesex, England

First published by Roc, an imprint of New American Library,
a division of Penguin Putnam Inc.

First Printing, March 2001
10 9 8 7 6 5 4 3 2 1

Cover art: Rick Lieder
Cover design: Ray Lundgren

 REGISTERED TRADEMARK—MARCA REGISTRADA

Printed in the United States of America

*This is for Brendan,
my Jackie Chan buddy and the
only sane one in the family*

# Previously, in *Black Oak*

A litmus test for those who would work with Ethan Proctor at Black Oak Investigations . . . and for some of those who use its services:

"Do you believe in ghosts?"

In Hart Junction, Kansas, Proctor and Vivian Chambers discover curious shards of what looks to be yellow glass in a ranch house where they both nearly lost their lives. Tests prove the glass to be an unidentifiable form of amber crystal. According to the test report, the shards are what's left of a globe, its size undetermined.

In a private jet over Virginia, Taylor Blaine hires Proctor and his firm to find his daughter, Celeste.

"Thirteen years, Proctor. She's been missing thirteen years, and I'll pay anything to find her again."

Celeste Blaine was last seen driving away from

her Connecticut home with her two best friends, Maude Tackett and Ginger Hong. They were eighteen, on their way to their freshman year at college.

No bodies were ever found.

Neither was the car.


In Pludbury, England, in a mansion called Beale Hall, Taylor Blaine sees a photograph of his daughter.

It is much less than ten years old.

When he brings Proctor in to see it as well, the photograph has vanished.

"But I saw it," Blaine insists. "I'm old, but I'm not senile. I saw it."


In Atlantic City, Proctor meets a beautiful woman named Petra Haslic.

He has no idea if she is human or not.

It doesn't matter; he cannot forget her.


*do you believe in ghosts?*

# ONE

*In the Pines . . .*
   . . . a breeze moves among the widely spaced trees like the current of a late-summer stream— lazily, easily, in no hurry to get from one place to another. Eddies of it near the ground for a moment spin dead leaves, or stir mounds of brown pine needles, or cause low weeds to quiver and let loose their seeds. Tufts of grass sway as though underwater; a fallen pinecone trembles; the feathers on a dead sparrow move not at all.

   The trees are white pine, their boughs thick and heavy. The lowest ones soon snap at the bole and add their bulk to the woodland floor, while the highest ones form an interlocking canopy that allows the afternoon sun to reach the ground only in patches that shift erratically as the day passes from dawn to dusk. Not much grass, then, and little concentration of underbrush; languid ferns and the occasional thorned thicket; temperatures not as warm as the piedmont that surrounds it, and autumn cold at night, even on the hottest day.

There is quiet, but it is not silent. The breeze sees to that, and the movement of birds and animals and the infrequent hiker who's taken a wrong turn in his walking tour of Burline County. The voice of the forest.

Peaceful, for the most part. Comfortable.

The breeze also carries with it the scent of the woods itself, and the fresh growth of a new spring, the warmth of the sunlight, loam and new blossoms vivid in the dim air, red earth and black dirt, and behind a solitary spindly thicket the old blood and rot of a fawn torn to pieces. Partially devoured.

*In the pines . . .*

. . . near their eastern boundary is a man-high boulder sunk into a shallow depression as if it had fallen from a star. Its dark rough surface is cut by lightninglike white cracks; a veil of moss on one side, a tiny blade of grass growing from a thimble-size hollow in the other. At the base, the depression is filled with a tangle of dead weeds, twigs and brown needles, clots of dirt, and a single thin white stick that looks remarkably like bone.

Five minutes later it still looked like bone, and Royal Blondell grunted softly. He sat cross-legged in front of the great rock, coonskin cap pushed back on his head, one eye half-closed as if that, somehow, would improve his vision and concentration. He rocked slowly forward, rocked slowly back, swayed slowly side to side before settling again. This was his routine, studying the protrusion from as many angles as possible without actually touching it. He wasn't uncomfortable; he had done this a million times, and he was in no hurry at all.

"Damn, Royal," his best friend, Garber, had once told him, "if we all worked like you do, we'd still be hunting for the first dinosaur bone."

Royal had only shrugged. Point of fact, he had little use for the academic we's of this world—except old Garber, of course. Sure, they wanted to learn and discover and figure things out, just like him, but it seemed like they ended up spending half their time working just as hard trying to find someone to pay for their expeditions, their excavations, all those new scientific gizmos to make the work easier. And get their names in the paper.

He, on the other hand, had no big degrees, no string of unpronounceable silly-looking abbreviations after his name. A high school diploma, nothing more, and proud of it. And a small inheritance from his mother to take care of his simple life, without anyone butting in.

A moth landed on the boulder, pale wings quivering.

Behind him some distance, he heard a couple

of birds arguing, voices carrying a slight echo in the trees. It made the woods seem that much bigger. That much more empty.

One day, around his twenty-third birthday, he got tired of pumping gas in Alton. It didn't seem like this was any way to live a life. So he quit, sat on his front porch for a couple of days, contemplating and figuring, then drove over to the high school after the last bell had rung. He made his way to Garber Kranz's classroom, and said, "Garb, the hell with it, I want to be an archeologist."

To his credit, Garb hadn't laughed. He only said, "Why?"

"'Cause I'm tired of stinking of grease and gas."

Royal grinned at the memory. No grease and gas now, just twelve years of dust and dirt and age and a few things he'd just as soon not remember. Not one second of which he would trade for anything.

The moth left; the birds fell silent. And finally, convinced he would disturb nothing important, do no irreparable harm to the site, he dug into the backpack lying on the ground beside him and pulled out an old but expensive pair of chef's tongs padded with soft rubber. He reached out to snare the bone and gently tugged at it. It was loose, and he tugged again, pulled it free, and held it up, head cocked, squinting.

"Y'know," he said with a rueful smile and sigh, "you can be dumber than a post sometimes, boy. Maybe you need your sorry eyes checked."

What he held was nothing more spectacular than a long twig with its bark recently stripped, not long enough in the air for the wood to darken, except at the bud knobs, which could be taken for small knuckles.

A morning and most of an afternoon wasted.

Still, he couldn't expect to hit pay dirt every time. If he did, what would be the fun of it? Where would be the adventure? Come up with a treasure every time he waved his trowel or spade, the whole thing would become downright . . . boring. And the one thing he could say about his life 'til now was, it sure as hell wasn't boring.

A little lonely sometimes, but that ain't the same thing.

"Up, boy," he muttered. "Your bones'll settle. They'll be digging you up next."

Another look at the twig, and he tossed it over his shoulder, packed the tongs away, and rose easily, slinging the pack into place. A stretch of each leg, each arm, his back and neck, and he settled his cap where it belonged. Then he slapped at the dust gathered on his baggy army pants and dark green shirt, checked to be sure nothing had fallen from the pockets, and decided maybe it was time he headed on home.

Maybe, in fact, he ought to hurry a little.

He had a feeling he was pressing his luck. Gone from his house for almost a week, tramping around, doing his work . . . yeah, maybe he was pressing his luck a little.

More often than not Royal wasn't a superstitious man, but he couldn't help it when he was here, in the pines. The spotlights of sunlight, the serenity, the way the air held glittering bits of dust, the way footsteps were cushioned by layers of fallen needles . . . it should have retained that pleasantly surprised sense of reverent awe he had felt when he'd first discovered it.

It should have.

It didn't.

As he walked eastward, following a trail only he could see, he glanced over his shoulder. Nothing there, of course. There never was. But it *felt* like it. Back there where the light didn't quite touch the ground, where the ferns resembled hands reaching out of the earth, something should have been there. Watching him. Measuring him. It was a foolish idea. A man of his experience ought to know better. Nevertheless, he gripped the backpack's straps and moved a little faster.

What he would do, he figured, is get himself home and have a good bath. Then something to eat while he watched TV to catch up on the news he'd missed the past six days. Then get on the phone and try to find Garb.

He scowled.

Garber was a man of strong habit, especially since he had retired from teaching. He would make a schedule for each day and stick to it. But every once in a while, as if one of his internal circuits got shorted, he would drop everything and light out of town. One year it was up to Myrtle Beach to play three days' worth of miniature golf; one time it was over to Savannah to sit by the river and throw rye bread to the gulls; last time it was to use a dugout Royal had made for him, paddling into the Okefenokee to, he claimed, track down Pogo and discover the Meaning of Life.

This was the first time, however, that he'd left town without slipping a message under Royal's welcome mat, letting him know where he had gone.

Royal huffed, and adjusted his pack. A line of sweat gathered around the rim of his cap, and he could feel his thin black hair matting to his scalp. As he topped a low rise, a stitch in his side made him grunt. He was startled he'd been traveling so rapidly. He stopped and leaned against a bole, bending over, bracing his hands on his knees. He sniffed and spat, spat again and scolded himself for acting like a frightened kid.

Still . . .

He looked to his right, saw how the pines began to give way to bulky oaks and fat-waisted cedar, a few twisted tall sycamore, long-limbed maple with scars in their bark. More grass, more underbrush. More light. He could see large fragments of darkening sky and the pale, almost transparent rise of an early-evening moon.

Word had it there was a pack of wild dogs making the rounds of the county. Some livestock chewed up, a couple of kids missing. This, he thought, would be a good place for the pack to hunt.

Great; a real good way to keep your nerves, you fool.

He began to hum an old folk song, one his momma used to sing. Used to be he thought it some kind of love song, some poor guy wondering why the lady he loved wasn't around anymore. Used to be that's what he thought.

*In the pines*

He looked left.

*In the pines*

Not any longer.

*Where the sun never shines*

Night had already arrived in the white pine forest, and with it the certain knowledge that he wasn't alone.

Fool, he thought, but that didn't stop him from shifting quickly from a walk to a trot, heading for the dirt road just a half mile away where he'd parked his old station wagon just after dawn. He couldn't remember the next line, but it didn't matter. Dumb song anyway.

Fool, he thought again, but he didn't look back.

And he didn't look up, in case he'd see the moon.

Darker now; so much darker.

The backpack thumped heavily against his spine; his left knee began to ache, legacy of a serious twist he had given it a few years back; it felt as if a hair had settled in his throat, and he finally began to cough, causing him to stumble and veer back and forth off the trail as if he were liquored. He spat, and coughed, and spat again hard, cleared his throat so many times it began to burn. Coughed and spat, wiped an arm over his eyes to clear away the sweat, blinding him just long enough to miss the way the ground dipped sharply and rose again, throwing him forward onto his hands and knees, his head so low he scraped his chin against a rock. A curse, as strong as he could make it, as he flailed upright. Looking back.

Darker; so much darker, and the moon so much stronger.

He wasn't sure, he wouldn't swear to it, but up there on the rise he'd left only a few minutes ago he thought he saw something weave among the trees . . . something low to the ground, russet and black. Following him.

Fox, he thought, but it was too damn big.

Calm gone and daylight nearly so, he ordered himself to run like hell, and so he did, seeing the road up ahead, not feeling anything but his legs and his arms and the weight on his back, the air like fire in his lungs.

With mouth and eyes wide he tripped through a patch of ivy onto the road, panicked for a second before he spotted the wagon only a few yards away, roof and rear bumper gleaming in the moonlight. He had to grab the door handle to stop himself from going too far, yanked the door open and threw the pack inside, fell behind the wheel and slammed the door closed behind him.

He sat for a moment, then used a fist to slam down all the locks; another moment to scrabble the keys from his pocket, jab the right one into the ignition and fire it, laughing aloud at the sound, laughing louder when he punched on the headlamps and watched the early night retreat into the woods.

"You're an idiot!" he yelled as he gripped the wheel and gunned the engine.

"You're an idiot," he whispered, as the adrenaline faded and shame at his panic took its place. "Idiot. Idiot."

He tossed his cap into the back and took his foot off the accelerator. "In the pines, my sorry ass." This was definitely something he would not tell Garb. No sense compounding his foolishness by giving his old friend a fresh target for some ribbing.

When he was sure he could drive without driving into the nearest tree, he said, "Home, you idiot, get yourself some food," and frowned slightly when his breath fogged the windshield.

He blew lightly, blew again, and wondered how it was possible the temperature had dropped so much so rapidly. Like goddamn winter, for God's sake, and he reached for the heater just as something, something large, slammed into the station wagon's back, snapping his head forward to slam against the steering wheel.

He didn't bother to look.

All he could do was drive, and pray that the old crate still had some speed.

All he could do, out here in the pines.

Where you shiver when the cold wind blows.

# TWO

Deep blue skies, a comfortably cool breeze, puffs-of-smoke clouds taking their time drifting out toward the Atlantic. Below the New Jersey Palisades a tour boat sails up the Hudson River toward West Point; a silent silver airliner heads low for the airport at LaGuardia; along the top of the cliffs low, thick evergreen shrubs, yew and hemlock, tremble as something small races through them, chittering softly to itself.

New flowers, new foliage, the smell of overturned earth in new gardens.

The overhead sun warms the low redwood deck only fifteen feet from the shrubs. A young jay sits on the railing for a few seconds before twitching its tail and vanishing in a flurry of dark blue and vivid white. A crow talks to its shadow on the pitched roof as it preens beneath its wings. Somewhere in the neighborhood a ball meets a bat, no sound like it in the world; all that's missing is the roar of a crowd.

A car horn; a little girl shrieks into giggles; on the other side of the long single-story house, hammering and inventive swearing.

It is about as perfect a spring day as a day can be in northern New Jersey, the eighth day of April, the second day of the week.

"I'm telling you right now," said Ethan Proctor, nodding toward the river a hundred feet below the cliffs, "if a pair of goddamn chipmunks jumps on the damn railing and starts singing and tap-dancing, I'm going to jump. I swear to God, I'm gonna jump."

He sat with his back to the house, jeans, a dark long-sleeve shirt rolled up twice at the cuffs, a pair of sunglasses that hid his eyes. A quick quiet laugh to his right, and he swiveled his head slowly. Eriko Nagai sat near the door that led into the living room. In her lap, a large legal pad; on the floor by her feet, a dozen folders. Her head was down, shoulder-length, gleaming black hair parted in the middle covering her face. Three fingers of one hand tried to hide her grin. Despite reminders that jeans or slacks were perfectly acceptable, she wore as always a loose white blouse and a black mid-calf skirt.

"I heard that," he told her sourly, turning back to face the river. He did not let her see the smile, quick as a breeze, touch a corner of his mouth.

"If you're going to jump," a woman said,

"please do it now so we can go home early. I'll call the cops on the way."

Again to his right, chair back to the railing, Lana Kelaleha shuffled envelopes in her lap, no expression on her face. Her hair was as black as Eriko's, but not nearly as long, with square bangs that covered her brow. She was Proctor's office manager without the official title, a magician whose skills and tricks were centered on her computers.

Eriko laughed again, very softly, but she didn't reveal her face. After nearly two months at Black Oak, she still wasn't sure what was proper behavior in front of her employer. He knew this, and made no attempt to make her more comfortable. She had seen just about all his moods, dark and light; she would either get used to them, or she would leave.

Hammering from the other side of the house, and a fresh round of swearing—Paul Tazaretti, repairing the steps on the small back porch. He had just finished an assignment and was, he claimed, using the good weather to make sure they didn't kill themselves trying to get to their cars.

"For crying out loud, can't we find him something else to do?" Proctor pleaded.

Lana shrugged. "He's fixed his Jeep, the electric door on the garage, and the garbage disposal. He's mowed the grass and, at your suggestion, rearranged the living room, then changed it back. Again, at your suggestion. He was talking about checking the roof, but I told him the insurance didn't cover it."

"That's not what I meant."

Lana gave him no answer. There were no other cases; at least none for Paul.

Black Oak's primary work was investigating financial scams and schemes, from a simple skimming off the top of someone's profits, to deceptions buried deeper in a company's books. Taz's youth and mechanical abilities enabled him to get dirty, to work with the troops, as he put it, become one of them and, eventually, learn their secrets, if there were any to be learned. The more complicated affairs, the ones requiring dealings with men who prowled large offices in tailored suits, and who often imagined themselves above suspicion, beyond reach . . . those clients were handled by Doc Falcon.

The problem was, Doc was still recovering from a harrowing incident last February down in Atlantic City. He had nearly been killed. He had lost an eye. Although under doctor's orders to rest, he had begun to visit the office now and then, bored and anxious, patient and resigned.

"I rather like the piratical look," he had declared the day before, indicating his black patch with the flick of a well-manicured finger. "Perhaps I should acquire a pegleg to complete the ensemble."

"It would ruin the line of your suit."

"I know. More's the pity."

They sat on the deck, watching nothing in particular, saying very little.

Finally, Proctor had snapped a thumb toward the house, asked him, "Are you ready?"

Doc had answered, simply, "No."

It was more than the pain, more than learning how to deal with diminished perception of distance and dimension. It was learning firsthand how to deal with a world he had only known before from stories and reports, had faced only in the most marginal, least threatening ways.

Now he had been thrust into Proctor's world, and now he had the dreams.

Proctor sighed and stretched out his legs, crossing them at the ankles. "All right, where were we?"

"Complaining about dancing chipmunks," Eriko said, sounding as if she were being strangled as she worked hard not to laugh again.

"I am suspicious," he told her with mock solemnity, "of perfect days, young lady. They lend themselves to uncontrolled explosions of joy, and feed the unreasonable hope that this is the day your numbers will hit and lottery millions are yours. Disappointment is inevitable. The future is dashed on the rocks of reality."

"Dash away all you want," Lana said, fanning three envelopes in her hand, "but these have very nice checks from three very nice families who, for the time being, think you walk on water. The bills, also for the time being, will be paid."

He almost smiled. "Murray."

She nodded.

Aside from the fact that Doc had survived, two very good things had resulted from the Atlantic City trip: One was extremely personal, and Proctor never spoke of it; the other was the result of an impulse—he had asked a newly retired, newly turned sixty New York City police detective named Murray Cobb to join the organization. Cobb had said he'd think about it, but only a week had passed before he showed up at the door.

"Retirement ain't what it's cracked up to be," he'd said by way of explanation. "I no sooner got home, I started counting the flowers on the wallpaper. I figured that was a sign."

As it turned out, despite his somewhat rumpled appearance and often brusque manner, he knew how to charm ladies of a certain age, no matter what their station. They trusted him instinctively and instantly, while Doc and his impeccable manner and clothes often tended to intimidate.

Lana stared at the house, not really seeing it, thinking. "He's in Wilmington again today. The way he works, we'll probably have another check in the morning."

Proctor shook his head in pleased amazement. "The Lord giveth, the Lord taketh—"

"Stop it!" she snapped, abruptly angry. "You're acting as if Doc's never coming back. He is. You know he is, and I will not have you thinking otherwise." She leaned toward him as if ready to leap from her chair, shaking the envelopes at him. "You can't . . . it wasn't your idea for that trip, it was mine. And if I thought for one second he wasn't going to—"

"All right," he said quietly, and she fell back, breathing heavily, swallowing hard. He kept his voice low. "It was a stupid thing to say. I didn't mean it. I wasn't thinking."

"Sorry," she whispered.

"No need."

She nodded, but didn't speak.

He looked then to Eriko, who was clearly startled by the exchange. "As you have no doubt already discovered," he said lightly, "being the daughter of a Mexican father and a Hawaiian mother has given Lana a somewhat strong and volatile personality, not to mention being married to a guy that's built like . . ." He stopped, shook his head slowly at his stupidity, took off his sunglasses. "Lana, do me a favor and give those checks to Taz, have him drop them at the bank. We'll do the rest of the mail later." A gesture kept Eriko in her seat.

When they were alone, he turned his chair around to face her, tucked the sunglasses into his breast pocket.

Above them they could hear the click of the crow's talons as it strutted across the roof. There was nothing else; the neighborhood had gone silent.

He watched her fuss with her pad, watched her tuck a strand of hair behind her ear, watched her do anything to avoid looking at him.

"Eri," he said gently, and she finally met his gaze, fearful, puzzled. Just as gently: "It's been a hectic few weeks, I know. Doc, my mother—" A shrug, a sideways nod at the house. "The business."

The crow settled down.

"We need to talk, Eri, something I should have done right after you came on."

Her hands fluttered over the pad until he nodded a suggestion she put it on the floor. When she did, she folded her hands in her lap, kept her head up. Waiting. Only her posture betrayed her tension.

He kept his voice soft, low. "The first thing is, relax. You're doing a fine job. A wonderful job. To come in as quickly as you did so RJ could take her

classes . . . except for Murray, I don't think anyone has fit in as quickly as you have."

A small grateful smile, but the tension remained.

Soft, low: "I wasn't kidding when I said I
should have talked with you long before this.
There are facets to this office you need to understand. RitaJane does; everyone does. If you're
going to stay on, you need to, as well."

She stirred, stared at her hands. "Taz told me,
the first thing you asked him was if he believed
in ghosts." He saw the frown. "Is that right? Was
he kidding?"

"No," Proctor said flatly. "He wasn't kidding."

"Are you going to ask me?"

The crow moved again, and it sounded like the
soft talk of an old hall clock.

He glanced at his watch, then reached out and
covered her hands with one of his until they
stopped trembling. A moment longer before he
took the hand away and put the sunglasses back
on, shifted his chair back to its original position.
"My mother's doctor is going to call in a couple
of minutes. I'll probably have to leave for a while.
But tomorrow you and I are going to get together
in the morning, so I can make up for what I
should have done sooner."

Taking this as a signal she could leave, she
picked up her notepad and stood. A nervous
hand brushed across the front of her skirt. "Mr.

Proctor, RJ is going to be in tomorrow. Lana said I don't have to be in until after lunch."

He looked at her for several seconds before turning back to the river. "You come straight to me, understand?"

"Yes, Mr. Proctor."

"Proctor," he corrected.

A hesitation before the door opened and she left him alone with the sun and the crow.

Left him alone, watching the toy of a tour boat slip into the sparkles that dotted the water. Wondering about the passengers. Wondering what it would be like, to be one of them. To be normal.

# THREE

Royal did not look at the station wagon's damage when he arrived home. He put it in the carport, practically broke through the kitchen door in his haste to get inside, and spent the next several hours sampling the variety of beers stacked in the refrigerator.

He did not bother to eat.

He did not bother to take off his coonskin cap.

A deer, he told himself firmly as he tossed an empty can into the sink and fetched himself another; it was only a deer that didn't have the brains God gave him.

Or it could have been one of those wild dogs, having some fun on its own.

Hell, it could have been a falling branch for all he knew.

But his hands would not stop shaking, and no matter where he looked, his eyes would not stop focusing on that flash of russet and black, and every time a finger strayed across the small lump on his forehead, he felt the jolt of the collision, felt the station wagon rock on its ancient protesting springs.

Heard the glass shatter when the rear window blew in.

When at last he realized there was nothing in the house but him and the darkness that slipped out of the corners, he wandered into the small living room and turned on the television set to make a connection with the world. He didn't care what the program was; all he wanted was the flickering light and the sound. Then he pulled down the shades, yanked the curtains closed, double-checked all the locks on the doors and windows, and decided that the beer just wasn't going to cut it.

He knelt in front of the old pine cabinet on which the TV sat, opened the doors that had never fit quite right, and grabbed the nearest bottle, a gift Garb had presented him a few weeks back—paint-peeling moonshine fresh from its manufacturer in the Lakochebala swamp. After bringing it back to the sagging couch, it took him a while to figure out it was a twist-top, not a cork; it took a while longer to stop coughing and gasping after the first swallow.

Once he got the hang of it, however, even the shaking stopped.

*A deer* was the last thing he thought before he passed out.

\*   \*   \*

Burline County had never been in the lime-
light and preferred it that way. The land was
rolling flat, spotted with nothing so large as a
forest, just woods now and then of white pine
and yellow pine, live oak, and a few cypress,
some strays of other kinds just to make it inter-
esting; wandering creeks and shallow streams,
the Lakochebala swamp, crossroad towns,
farms that made up in produce what they
lacked in size, and orchards of pecan trees
whose size seldom failed to amaze tourists,
who usually thought the nuts grew on bushes.
Spotty white fields of cotton. Beef cattle and
one thriving horse ranch. Schools that made
sure their children's education remained above
the state average. Cable TV, tar-paper shacks,
churches that ministered to several hundred or
several dozen, Cadillacs and dusty pickups,
poachers and politicians.

A way of getting through life, of getting the
best out of life, without breaking a sweat, taxing
the heart.

And the almost universal belief that the natural world was often as good a teacher as anyone
in a university, that there wasn't a text in any
classroom that could rightly teach a youngster
how to make the poultice that drew the sickness
from someone's soul, how to read the weather in
the way the leaves danced and quivered, how to

smell danger on the wind that followed a crimson sundown.

But no one knew how to read the corpse of a prime stud bull whose massive head had been nearly torn from its shoulders. No one understood a pair of disemboweled plow horses just one season away from heading out to pasture.

When Cank Howard's body was found on the north shore of the Lakochebala, enough critters had been at it that it had been difficult at first to understand how the old bum had died . . . until the autopsy revealed that someone, something had ripped him open and shredded his heart.

The initial reaction to the alleged disappearance of John Verlin and Sissy Brock was an amused-mixed-with-relief belief the two had finally given up on their feuding families and eloped to a more amenable climate . . . until John was found tangled in the roots of an old cypress on Union Creek. Tangled because there was very little left holding him together.

Sissy was still missing.

So was Maudie Batts, the county's only self-proclaimed witch, a young woman who relied on crystals and the tarot, scented candles and spell books from England, and several trips to Arizona to keep her in touch with the spirit world when she wasn't managing Toad Hall, a book- and toy store on the square in Alton, the county seat.

Still, the pack of wild dogs theory persisted until the last day of March, when Spence Durban, grey-haired deacon in the Holy Temple of God Chapel, was found in the church's graveyard, draped over his wife's headstone. His throat and chest had been savaged, and in his right hand was a .357 Magnum. There were no bullets left in the clip, and every shell had been accounted for. Durban was known countywide for being a damn good shot, even with a weapon as powerful as the Magnum. If he aimed at it, he generally hit it.

There was no other body but his; there was no other blood but his. The only prints in the soft earth were his, not a sign of a dog pack anywhere. Just a single pawprint fifteen yards away, and no one wanted to speculate on how large a dog would have to be to leave a print that big. Or how Spence, even in a panic, managed to miss it all those times.

They did anyway.

"I'm telling you, Royal," Deke Spangler declared, holding his left hand over his head, "the son of a bitch has to be eight, nine foot high, easy."

"Oh, please," said Connie Plaine, who was anything but. "And I'm gonna be Miss September next year, birthday suit and all." She gave the big man a disgusted, *lay off the fish story* look and patted Royal's arm. "It's pretty bad, though, Royal. There's no official curfew, anything like that, but you'd never know it around here."

Royal said nothing. His head was about to explode like a popped balloon, his stomach stubbornly refused anything that even hinted at nourishment except the cup of black coffee in front of him, and he hadn't yet been able to understand how all this had happened while he had been traipsing around the damn woods. The bull and horses he had heard about; it was the murders that were new.

When he had groaned awake that morning, cursing Garber and the moonshine, he had taken his time putting himself back together. Once dressed, in a loose cotton shirt and baggy jeans, he dithered for a while before finally checking on the station wagon's condition. As soon as he saw the indentation in the pull-down door, the jagged pieces of glass, the smashed taillight, he knew damn well it was no deer that had hit him. Yet, despite his hangover, he had gone quickly into what he called his "recover and discover" mode—he grabbed his camera and took pictures from as many angles as he could, inside and out; he drew a couple of sketches; then he studied the damage up close, looking for anything that might give him a clue as to what the hell he was looking at.

Right now, in his kitchen, he had two sealed

plastic bags: One held a tuft of what looked like hair or fur, the other protected three shards of glass that looked as if they'd been stained with blood.

"Royal?" It was Connie, touching his arm lightly, bringing him back to the world. "Royal, you okay?"

Once he was sure he had collected all the evidence there was to collect, he drove straight to Spangler's Body Shop, where Deke took one look at the wagon, one look at him—"Damn, boy, you look like a goldfish about to go belly up"—and announced an early lunch break. Ignoring all objections, he manhandled Royal to the Pecan Express, one of Alton's several eateries on the streets surrounding the town square. They hadn't been there five minutes when Connie had seen them through the window and joined them.

When they learned he had been out on one of his digs, they took turns filling him in on what he had missed, and as his hangover subsided, he became increasingly convinced that whatever had killed poor old Durban had been after him too.

"So what is it?" he asked hoarsely, cleared his throat, and sighed relief when his stomach growled. A quick raised hand stopped his friends from answering, and at the same time brought Polly Dove to the booth, order pad in hand, shy smile on a pink-cheeked thin face made remarkable in Royal's opinion, and in spite of her last name, by huge brown puppy-dog eyes.

The day she had started work, Royal had made it a point to eat here once a week, no more, no less, when he was home. It hadn't taken long to progress from "How do you like your eggs?" to "I know, I know, no mustard on the burger."

He had never found the nerve to ask her out, though he sure as hell wanted to, because he knew someone like her wasn't about to be seen, in public or otherwise, with someone like him. A man who dug up bones.

Once he had given his order and passed a few words about the weather, he asked his friends again: "So what was it?"

Deke's broad shoulders rose in a slow shrug. "Cops are still saying it's those damn dogs." He leaned forward, clasping his hands on the table, those big hands and bigger arms looking for all the world like a double-handle sledgehammer. "Myself," he said, glancing around the crowded room, keeping his voice low, "I think it's one of those mass killers, you know? Got himself some kind of tool to cut people up with."

Connie snorted derision; Deke didn't take offense. He only shrugged again and sat back, smiling politely when Polly delivered Royal's lunch, gave him a sad look and hurried away.

"Sweet on you," Deke said, grinning. A wink: "She's jealous of Connie here, doesn't like the competition."

"You like to hear yourself talk, don't you?" Connie said. But her cheeks had colored slightly and she began fussing unnecessarily with her curly blond hair. She wore a white uniform, signature of her status in Dr. Oraden's clinic just around the corner. The gossip had been that the former Miss Burline County would have him hogtied at the altar six months after she'd taken the job; that was two years ago, and half the bachelors in the county had begun circling again.

"I speak," Deke answered, still smiling, "with the voice of authority."

Royal only half listened to their friendly bickering. The burger seemed to be staying down, and for that he was grateful. What he had to do after lunch was figure a way to get someone to test the samples he had found that morning. It was probably nothing, no matter what he'd thought earlier, but there was no sense leaving anything to chance. If it turned out to be a deer after all—Praise God—he would find a way to turn the whole episode into a story he could take drinks on for months.

Kidding yourself, fool, he thought as he moved from the burger to the fries; kidding yourself.

He blinked when Deke laughed in that wheezing kind of way he had, and half turned so he could see Connie better.

"What did you just say?"

She glared at Deke to keep him quiet, lowered her head a little and leaned closer. "I've just been listening to some of Dr. Oraden's patients the last couple of days, that's all."

"Superstitious idiots," Deke muttered. "Gives the South a bad name is what they do."

"About what?" Royal said.

Connie leaned closer still. "I'm not saying I believe this, mind, but they're saying it's one of those shape-shifter things, you know?"

Royal swallowed a laugh. "You're kidding."

"Look," she said defensively, straightening, meeting his gaze head-on, "these are poor folks, you understand what I mean? They use the clinic because it's mostly free, they can't afford it otherwise. So living where and how they do, they have a different perspective on life than us."

"Oh, Jesus," Deke said in disgust, and looked out the window at the pedestrian traffic. "Give us a break here, huh?"

Royal waved him silent. "So you're saying they're talking about what, a werewolf or something?"

After a moment's hesitation, she nodded. "Or someone who thinks he is."

"And how do they figure that?"

She leaned back and stared at the ceiling fans for a few seconds, clearly trying to decide how much she should say. Then she leaned over the table, forcing the others to lean with her so they could hear:

"Dr. Oraden does the autopsies, you know that, right? Well, last night I was working late doing some filing and stuff, I happened to see a report on his desk." Her expression dared them to interrupt; neither man took it. "They weren't just all 'cut up,' and we're talking about the animals here, too." She took a breath. "They were partially devoured."

Royal didn't know what to say, how to respond, so he rearranged his silverware, took a sip of his now cold coffee, and finally looked up at Deke, who had gone considerably pale.

"I . . . I have to go," Connie said, gathering up her purse and check. "I have to—"

And Royal said, "Damn!"

The chill he felt had nothing to do with the air-conditioning.

"What?" Deke said.

Royal gestured vaguely, almost frantically. "Garber. Garb is missing."

# FOUR

There were times when, if Proctor thought about it too long, he would feel superfluous in his own house, at his own business. In many ways it should have been a compliment to the way he had organized Black Oak without actually setting limits in stone. He knew this, but there were still times . . .

He sat in the living room, in a claw-footed wingback chair that Taz once said could have been some monarch's throne if it hadn't been so damn ugly. To his right, most of the wall was covered by a bookcase fronted by etched-glass doors. He faced a walnut coffee table in front of a long, three-cushion couch, with two not-quite-respectable end tables and a pair of overstuffed armchairs. Beyond the couch was the dining room, with a table that seated eight, and beyond that a picture window that looked out on the backyard and the screen of Douglas firs that hid the house from the street.

Up the hall to the right he heard voices: Lana explaining some managerial esoterica to Eriko, while RJ wanted to know who had screwed up her supply-room system again. When last heard from this morning, Murray was on his way home with a check, and a fat bonus from a grateful client; to escape RJ, Taz had volunteered to drive downtown for doughnuts from the Swiss bakery; Doc hadn't come in.

Proctor shifted, one foot beating slow time to music only he could hear.

Two messages had been left on the answering machine while he had showered that morning, both telling him to expect calls later in the day. The first he had already received—Paul Browning, his mother's doctor, wanted him to know that there had been a couple of subtle changes in her condition over the past few days.

"Nothing I can point at and say, 'Hey, look,'; it's more a feeling, I guess. But it's there, Proctor. It's there."

Sometimes Proctor lost count of the years that had passed since his mother had fallen into a kind of catatonia. Her eyes were open but no one knew what she saw; she sat when directed; she ate when directed; she never smiled, never frowned, never made a sound. Last January she had said her first words— "tiger's eye"—since the condition set in, and

now something else. A feeling, not much more.
But something else.

It would help if they knew what had caused
the condition in the first place. But no one did.
Only his mother.

The second message was from Vivian Chambers, and it took all the control he had not to pick
up the phone and call her back.

"Big doings, Proctor," she had said. "I'll be in
touch later, but for God's sake don't call, you
might screw it up."

His foot tapped a little more quickly.

There had been no hint of promise or despair
in her voice, but it had to be about Taylor Blaine,
for whom she served as both confidante and
bodyguard. For months the old man had been in
such a deep depression over the lack of progress
in finding his missing daughter that his remaining children had taken over the old man's company. A coup. And Black Oak had been one of the
casualties.

He stared at the telephone on the coffee table.
What would he screw up if he called? Taylor was
a friend as well as a client; where was the harm?
He pushed a rebellious shock of dark sandy hair
from his brow; the fingers of his left hand provided counterpoint on the chair's arm to the beat
of his foot; he made to stand, settled back, and refused to look at his watch.

Where was the harm?

He hadn't seen Vivian in several weeks. She had said nothing to him then about the situation, had given him no reason to hope. There was nothing left but to trust her.

Eriko walked out of the hall, placed an armful of folders on the dining-room table and neatened the pile. Humming softly she turned, gasped, and slapped a hand against the flat of her chest.

"Sorry," she said. "I . . . I didn't see you there."

He pointed at the couch. "Have a seat, Eri. It's time."

After an apprehensive look up the hall, she nodded quickly and sat in the middle of the center cushion, hands in her lap, knees together, feet flat on the floor. Despite Lana's instructions, she had arrived with RJ just before ten. Too nervous, he figured, about staying home.

He felt the late-morning sunlight at his back, spreading around the chair to capture her in brightness, leave him in shadow.

"You stayed up all night worrying."

Her head tilted in a shrug, an admission.

"You'll drive yourself crazy if you try to read my mind."

No movement this time.

"Lana," he called. When she appeared, he nodded to Eri. "Stay away for a while. Tell RJ."

She frowned, but his look turned her around and sent her back to her office.

Then he watched Eriko for a full silent minute, impressed at the way her unease and curiosity showed only in the unnatural stiffness of her spine.

Too young, he thought suddenly. Although she, like RJ, was in her early twenties, he couldn't help feeling she was a lot younger than that.

"As I said yesterday," he told her, his voice quiet, "I should have done this a long time ago. I can't tell now if it's too late or not. It is entirely your decision, once we're finished." A single finger raised to forestall interruption. "Things are suddenly happening quickly around here. Too quickly for me sometimes, and I'm the one who knows everything that's going on. This is important, Eri. There is no room for telling me what you think I want to hear. When we finish, it's your move."

He waited a few seconds to get a sense of her, to see if she was inclined to bolt, or to demand explanations.

She waited.

He nodded.

"You already know about Doc's . . . injury. You've probably seen the report filed for the record, and Taz has probably filled in some of the more, as Murray would say, lurid details." He lowered his head and thought for a moment. "I'm telling you right now, that official report, the one in Lana's office, is a lie. The one in my office isn't."

Her head jerked, just a little, the only sign the rippling of her hair.

"You know too about the other cases, not Murray's or Doc's. Mine. The private ones. You've also probably wondered why I'm the one who goes after the charlatans, those dead-hearted sons of bitches who 'talk to the spirits,' play at ghost and monster so they can make a few miserable bucks off people who don't know any better." He looked up then, gave her a brief, one-sided smile. "You don't really understand, and probably think I'm a little nuts. You've even maybe wondered if the pay is good enough to keep you working around people like us."

She shifted, but didn't look away.

He kept his voice gentle. "It's all right, Eri. Everyone has felt that way in the beginning. A few have quit, and that's all right too." A long steady look. "But now it's my turn."

She sat straighter, more uncertainty in her eyes, in the way her hands began to move in her lap.

"There was a family," he said, and with that statement, in sunlight and shadow, they were the only two people in the house, in the town, in the world.

"They lived in Michigan. They wanted to move

into a house the husband's great-grandfather had built shortly after the Civil War. Although the house meant a great deal to these people, the locals discouraged them from the beginning, saying the place was unsafe, too many repairs and upgrades were needed, the back taxes were prohibitive, and anyway, it was haunted by the old man himself, and he wasn't very friendly.

"The husband didn't believe it, of course. He paid the back taxes and spent tens of thousands bringing the house into the twentieth century. He had to use imported labor because none of the local craftsmen would take a job anywhere on the property. Dangerous, haunted—the same excuses every time.

"Predictably, the accidents began. Not serious ones, just curious ones. Tools began to disappear. Repairs were undone. A few minor injuries. The local police made halfhearted efforts to find the thieves, and those who caused the accidents and vandalism, but they came up with nothing. When the accidents got worse, however, the injuries more serious, the wife contacted someone who eventually contacted me. She was afraid for her husband's and children's safety. She loved that old place, but she didn't want to die there before her time.

"I went out. I poked around. I made myself very unpopular. I discovered a codicil to the old man's will, which left the house and a whole lot of acres of prime land to the town the day his descendants gave up their claim to the family holdings. It doesn't matter who was guilty, and who eventually went to jail. The family won, finished the reconstruction, moved in, and every Christmas I get a card from them, with a picture of the house."

He leaned forward, out of the gloom.

"Eri, it's your turn now . . . do you believe in ghosts?"

"There was no ghost there, Mr. Proctor." She flinched. "Sorry. Proctor."

He sat back. "My last night, I walked from the house back to my motel. As I passed through these huge iron gates at the foot of the drive, I saw someone standing at the side of the road. He was under some trees, out of the moonlight, so I couldn't see him clearly. My first thought was that one of the bad guys was out for a little revenge. It wouldn't have been the first time.

"But I kept walking, kept looking over, and just after I passed him, he said, 'Thank you, sir. They were always greedy sons of bitches. And damn liars, too.'

"I stopped and turned, and he was gone. I ran over and saw no sign that anyone had been there at all. The trees were too thick, and I stood for a long time listening for movement in there. Then I went home."

He leaned forward again. "Do you believe in ghosts, Eri?"

She smiled at the story, his point made. She rose, smoothed the front of her skirt, and he waited. Wondering.

"Mr. Proctor, I am what my family calls *sansei*. Third generation in this country. My family . . . my grandparents on both sides were interred in Manzanar during the Second World War. They were very young, and when they were released they ran away from California, all the way to North Carolina, where my parents and I and my brothers and sisters were born. That's why I have an accent that kind of doesn't go with my face. My father calls it Nippon Southern. My mother doesn't think that's funny."

She hesitated; he didn't move.

"I graduated from Duke. Two days later I was in a park, sitting at a picnic table near a small pond. Lots of people around, a really nice day. Not too hot, you know? A nice cool breeze. The park was crowded, and I was feeling a little down. You know, all that work, all the study, and now it was over?" She shrugged. "I guess I was kind of sad."

She plucked at nothings on her skirt, brushed her hair from her eyes.

"Then a voice said my name, and I turned, and there was my uncle. My father's brother. I loved him when I was little, he was my favorite, but he and my father had had a big fight about something, I never knew what about, and he went away when I was ten. I never saw him again.

"He said, 'I see you've graduated. *Omedeto gozimasu*.'

"I was so happy to see him, I couldn't answer right away, and he smiled at me. He had this funny smile, I can't describe it, but he smiled, and said, 'How are you, Eriko?'

" 'Fine, *Ojii-chan*. Thank you.'

" 'You've done very well. I'm proud of you.'

"I thanked him again—I was so surprised he was there I still couldn't talk, all the questions I wanted to ask.

"Then he leaned over and the smile went away, and he said, 'You must know, *Eriko-chan*, that I will look out for you. I will help you when I can.'

"I wanted to ask him where he'd been all this time, and I guess I started to get a little angry, you know? My favorite uncle in all the world, and he just dropped out of my life. But before I could say anything, he asked me where I lived, so I turned around to point at this apartment building across the street from the park.

"When I turned back to see if he understood, he was gone. I jumped up and tried to find him in the crowd, but he was gone. Him and that silly little smile."

She shook her head, tilted it in a shrug, and headed for the hall, toward the office she shared with RJ. Then she stopped and turned around.

"Mr. Proctor, I didn't tell my father about him because he was still pretty angry after all those years. I asked my mother, I didn't tell her I'd seen him, and she said she was pretty sure my uncle had died during my freshman year."

Her smile was small; he couldn't read it.

"So I can't answer your question, Mr. Proctor. Because I don't really know."

When she was gone, he stared across the couch into the living room, to the green-shaded brass lamp that hung from the ceiling. There was no draft, but every so often, like now, it swayed a little. Just a little.

Finally, he nodded. Good enough, Eriko, he thought; good enough.

When Taz returned, the office instantly filled with the aroma of fresh hot pizza. Proctor stood in the doorway between the galley kitchen and the dining room, taking plates and silverware for distribution on the table.

"It was lunchtime," the younger man explained, "so I figured this was better than doughnuts, okay? Besides," he added, raising his voice, "it's better than eating organically grown lettuce crap like some people I know."

"It's good for you," RJ yelled back. "And if you touch my sausage and extra cheese, you're a dead man."

Proctor squeezed past him to the back door, listening to the others while he used a pizza slicer to finish the work the shop had begun. Once the food had been served, drinks poured, he waited until Taz returned to the kitchen, looking for him, eyes narrowed in puzzlement. "What? I forget something?"

"I want you to talk to Eri. Fill her in. Do it today, don't listen if Lana complains."

Taz pushed a hand back through his thick and wavy black hair. "Everything?"

Proctor nodded.

"You sure?"

"Yes." He moved to the sink, picked up the slicer and rinsed it under warm water. "Use your good sense. Don't push too hard, she won't be able to take it all in. But she has to know everything she can. After Doc . . ." He turned off the water, dried his hands with a paper towel. "She has to know, Taz. See to it."

Once at the table, he had just taken his first bite when someone slammed open the kitchen door. Startled, he was halfway to his feet when Vivian practically leapt into the room, breathing heavily, her long hair wind-tangled.

With a huge grin, she spread her arms wide, and said, "If I were working for you, Proctor, I'd demand a raise."

# FIVE

Clouds, high and thick, straight out of the Gulf of Mexico, stalled over the county and began to merge, killing the sunlight without lowering the temperature. The afternoon became muggy, tropical, and somewhere up there was the distant grumbling of thunder.

Royal paid the approaching storm little heed. He had bolted from the Express as soon as he'd paid his share of the check and, after flapping his arms helplessly once back on the sidewalk, he headed south at a pace that didn't take long to put sweat on his face. He ignored the shops and offices, only glanced with a distracted smile at the few people who greeted him. He wasn't a big man, not nearly as big as Deke, but those who didn't know him got out of his way quickly enough.

It pained him a little to see their expressions; they undoubtedly thought he was a crazy man, maybe a drunk, but there was nothing he could do about it. He had to get to Garber's place; after blurting what he had to his friends, he had to prove that he was wrong.

Devoured? Those poor people were partially eaten?

He crossed the street and was nearly clipped by a van, whose driver suggested loudly, and obscenely, that if he wanted to commit suicide, he should do it somewhere else.

Royal waved an apologetic hand and kept moving, more careful at the next corner, panting to a slow walk by the fourth. A bandanna from his hip pocket dried his face for the time being, a forearm over his hair to slick it away from his face. He was sorry now he had left the wagon at the body shop, but there was no time to retrieve it.

Shapeshifter?

Certainly not that, but it was certainly something. Several times a year there was an article in the *Burline Advocate* about the police having to pick up some bizarre pet or other from an outlying home. Once, it had been a mangy, virtually toothless black bear; escaped pythons showed up at least once a summer; and not all that long ago a family of nine was relieved of what it insisted was its guard dog—a very lean, very angry, and not-at-all-toothless panther, which had mauled a telephone lineman to death.

As he left the business area behind and turned

a corner into a neighborhood of small brick houses, he wondered if that was it. A panther. They were certainly close enough to Florida for one of those things to make its way north for a while. But no one had even brought it up.

Pecan and live oak provided spotty shade, but did nothing for the humidity, which had him moving even slower, gasping silently. Cursing himself for acting like an old man, he tried to push through it, failed, and had to lean against a stop sign for a breather.

The thunder was not quite so distant.

The bandanna again to his face and neck before he pushed off and carried on.

The neighborhood changed. The same kind of houses, though more of them were clapboard, more of them single-story, but the yards were not as large and not as well kept, more peeling shutters and railings, more older cars slumped in driveways. More empty lots.

Garber lived on a block that had only two other houses, both of them on the other side of the street. No sidewalks now, and the macadam was cracked and sprouting weeds near the verge. The area wasn't a slum but, as Garb had once put it, "a ragged slice of genteel poverty."

The house was old chipped brick, with a stoop for a front porch and a roof haphazardly repaired into a patchwork of shingle and tar paper. Yet the yard was neat, a few flowering shrubs carefully maintained, and at the head of the front walk a trellis of climbing roses, a challenge to get through when the bees were at work. Two sixty-foot pecan trees in the yard near the house made the place seem even smaller than it was.

There was no newspaper on the welcome mat, which Royal hoped was a good sign. He rang the doorbell, knocked, rang the bell again, and shaded his eyes so he could see through the small window in the center of the door.

No one answered, and he could see no one inside.

"Come on, Garb," he muttered. "Come on, come on."

Not caring that he might be seen and thought a burglar, he made his way around the house, peering through the windows, whose shades had all been drawn, hoping he could see something around the edges or at the bottom. There was no garage, nor was there a carport. Garb claimed his car was so old anything like that was a waste of good wood and money.

The car wasn't here either.

At the back door Royal knocked again, using his fist and calling out. When he still received no response he reached under the stiff-straw mat and retrieved the house key. He wasted no time getting inside, no time hurrying through the rooms, yelling Garber's name, demanding an appearance.

Nothing; he wasn't here. And the house had that empty, heavy, too warm feeling of being without its owner for more than a couple of days.

"All right," he said. "All right, fool, time to think."

He returned to the kitchen and stood at the back door, facing the room. Time for a dig. Time to use your head, take it one step at a time. See what you're looking at; understand what you're seeing. If you don't get it, figure it out.

He moved slowly now, checking cupboards and refrigerator—all full and the milk and orange juice were fresh, so he hasn't been gone all that long. No messages on the answering machine in the living room. No newspapers. No signs of snacks or frozen dinners. The bed wasn't made, but his friend never made it anyway, and he wouldn't know if any clothes were missing or not. An empty suitcase in the hall closet.

The last room was Garb's study, and that was hopeless because Royal wouldn't know what was normal here if his life depended on it. Books on shelves, books and magazines in tottering piles on the floor; papers on the desk, but they meant nothing to him.

An open folder did, however; in fact, it surprised him near to tears.

It was a collection of newspaper and magazine clippings, all about him. How he had worked from books and under Garber's tutelage to learn what he had; how he had traveled to Montana, California, the Southwest, working on and observing digs so he could study the methods firsthand; how he had discovered that small Seminole encampment in the Lakochebala, when it was thought the tribe hadn't come back this far north after finally settling in Florida; snippets and paragraphs about the fossils and settlement remains he had uncovered, on his own, here and in surrounding counties.

All of it; his life's work right here in this folder.

That stupid, wonderful son of a bitch had been keeping track of it all.

Another quick look around, but no sign of that unidentifiable, what looked like glass, thing he had found and brought back as a gift to his friend.

"Damnit," he said as he tromped back to the living room and dropped onto the couch. "Damnit, where the hell are you?"

Never before had Garb done this, but there had to be a good reason; it wasn't like they were married, for God's sake. It was, he decided, Deke's and Connie's fault, filling his head with all that talk about mass murderers and werewolves and God only knew what else. And how the hell could he have allowed himself to be so spooked in the woods yesterday?

There had to be a clue here, something he had missed.

He closed his eyes, retraced every step from the minute he had entered the house, watching himself as if he were watching a movie, concentrating on everything he saw. He had just reached the bedroom again when a detonation of thunder brought him to his feet with a holler.

The house was dark; lightning flared around the edges of the shades, and thunder exploded again. Rain slammed against the windows. Crannies in the eaves gave the wind a high-pitched angry whistle.

Disoriented, groggy, it took him a while to realize he had fallen asleep, and that made him angry. He marched to the front door and yanked it open, swearing at the warm wind that blew water into his face. Up the road, a single streetlamp illuminated a running river at the junction of verge and macadam, bright slashes of rain in the air.

A July thunderstorm in April, he thought sourly; just great. No way he'd be able to get back to Deke's place now and retrieve the wagon. By the looks of things this would only settle into a nightlong downpour, which meant he was stuck. Even if he called, Deke wouldn't budge. And he didn't want to give Connie the wrong idea.

That made him grin, the idea being so foolish, and he shook his head, grinned again when he realized how wet his jeans legs had gotten. His anger was gone. No big deal staying the night. Garb wouldn't mind.

Search parties had been out for those who were missing; tomorrow he would make sure one was organized for Kranz.

He stepped back and closed the door, worked the wall switch and shrugged when the lamps and overhead hall light didn't come on. He didn't need them anyway; he knew where the bed was, and he might as well get there now since, if the lights weren't working, the TV wouldn't either.

He was halfway to the bedroom when a thump against the door told him a tree branch had fallen. His first inclination was to ignore it. His second was that he'd better clear it off the stoop now because, the way his luck was going, he'd forget about it in the morning, go rushing out, trip over it, and break his neck falling down the stairs.

The house vibrated at the next lightning-and-thunder eruption, and as he grabbed the door-knob and turned it, he hesitated.

What if it's out there?

Perfect time for it; what if it's out there?

"For Christ's sake, Royal," he said angrily, and pulled the door open.

Rain lashed across the threshold; leaves writhed in the air; the streetlamp winked out, winked on again, weaker.

No branch on the stoop, or on the front walk, or on the lawn.

The rose trellis had tipped over, petals scattered on the street.

He blinked once when he felt the wind take him, first warm, then cool, then ice.

He blinked again when he saw it rushing at him from the darkness.

"Lord Jesus," he said as he backed away, one arm raised. "Lord Jesus."

He said nothing else, and there was no time to scream.

# SIX

They stood on the deck, Proctor and Vivian, shadows creeping over the edge of the cliff, the sun glaring in the windows of the tall buildings on the New York side of the river. A chilly breeze, but not unpleasant.

Over an hour since her decidedly uncharacteristic entrance, an hour for her news to be absorbed. Taz, definitely characteristically, demanded a celebration, seconded by RJ. Proctor had listened to them, watched them, then suggested, mildly, that they get back to work. RJ did her best to flounce from the room, but her height defeated her; Taz complained, but kept it under his breath; Eriko took Lana's lead and simply left, asking questions about the taxes due the following week.

Vivian had seen it before, the way he handled them. No; *handle* was the wrong word, but she couldn't think of a better one. Piece by piece, height and weight and features, he was not an imposing man. His manner, and those deep-set, sometimes unnerving eyes, did all the work for him. He never yelled, he seldom ordered, he simply . . . spoke, and things were done.

A look requested she join him out here, and she took a deep breath, closed her eyes, smelled the day's warmth leaving the wood and the air.

"Thank you," he said, not looking at her, hands in his jeans pockets.

"Glad to help."

This was difficult for him, taking Blaine's money, accepting cases Blaine steered his way. It had saved the company from going under. The old man's daughter was thirteen years gone, and she knew Proctor still hadn't given up, and was feeling guilty, or helpless, because he hadn't found her yet, or any indication she was still alive. A proud man. They were both proud men.

"I wish I had been there to see it."

She put her hands on the railing, rocked slowly back and forth. "He could have gone either way, Proctor. He could have fired me without thinking twice about it."

"No. I don't think so."

"You weren't there, remember?"

"Didn't have to be for that one."

She heard it then, the wish that he had been the one to break through. Blaine had been . . . somewhere else since finding his daughter's picture in England, somewhere else because no one else had seen it, only Proctor believing him. He had sunk so deeply into whatever it was that the twins, Franklin and Alicia, had effectively taken over the company. And in doing so had fired Black Oak as well.

"I kept at it, that's all," she said, taking no credit. "You weren't there all the time, I was."

Finally, yesterday afternoon, she had trampled her duties to the old man as friend and body-guard; she had lost it, started raising her voice which, she knew from experience, would only make him more stubborn. There in his huge second-story library on his Connecticut estate, she had reminded him, bitterly and sometimes vulgarly, of all the work Black Oak had done, how much they cared for him beyond his business-rescuing checks. Then her frustration, her exasperation, had grown to such an extent that she said two things that, in retrospect, should have forced him to throw her out.

She had leaned as close as she dared and said, "I saved your life, you owe me, Mr. Blaine. You *owe* me."

And:

"He's obviously getting somewhere, because someone's trying to kill him, and it doesn't have anything to do with some damn company drone dipping into some damn retirement fund. You haven't seen what I have, Mr. Blaine. You may think you've seen a ghost, but I've seen a hell of a lot worse."

By the time she had finished she was, for the first time in years, yelling and waving her arms; by the time she was done, she was so angry she had to walk away from him, stiff-legged, muscles close to cramping; by the time she was done, she was positive she would be packing her bags that very night.

She snapped open a pair of French doors and stepped out onto the balcony that overlooked the old man's holdings. She wanted to jump; she wished she could fly; she held up a fist and glared at it so she wouldn't cry.

Eventually she felt a stiff finger poke her spine.

"Vivian, we will make a deal. Right now."

She had nodded without turning around.

"You will never, ever, speak to me that way again."

Another nod.

"And I will let you listen in when I tell my children that their old man is back."


"The right place at the right time, that's all," she told Proctor. "A day earlier, probably, and I would be looking for a new job."

He turned to lean back against the railing, hands still in his pockets. A glance down the length of the extralong house; a glance at the darkening sky.

"I owe you one."

"No, it's all right. They were getting ready to ax me too, remember?"

Steady and low: "I owe you one."

All these months, all they had been through, she knew this was no gesture. It was a pact.

"All right."

"Thanks."

She bent over the railing, stomach pressed into the edge, to try to see what made the scurrying noises she heard underneath. The squirrels, probably. He fed them, encouraged them, not, she suspected, because he really liked them, but because they drove Lana up the wall.

Like the crow she could hear on the roof behind her. There were dozens of them in the neighborhood, but she was ready to swear that this was the same one every time. She didn't like it. Not the way it looked at her, not its rough voice, not the way it paraded around as if it owned the place. It had nothing to do with dire omens and obscure symbols; at least she didn't think it did. With Proctor, in his world, nothing was ever what it appeared to be.

A squawk, a flutter, and it landed on the railing between them. Proctor didn't move, but she heard him whisper, "Beat it," just before it flew away.

When she looked over she saw his lips barely form a smile, and not for the first time she wondered if he ever smiled normally instead of moving only one side of his mouth. This time she thought it was at her expense, and she called him on it.

"Deliberately?" he said, and shook his head. "You think I control him?"

"He left when you told him to."

"He's a bird. Voices bother him."

"He winked at me."

"Maybe he likes you."

"You wouldn't tell me even if you could, would you."

"Not a chance."

She nodded, mimicked his stance. "He wants a report," she said.

"He'll get one."

"I think he'll want to see you soon."

"Yeah. No problem. I want to see him, too."

To make sure he's all right, she thought; you don't want to lose him again.

He pushed away from the railing and faced her. "What did Franklin say?"

"Nothing."

His eyebrow cocked in disbelief.

"Really. He did a long speech on how pleased he and his sister were that Taylor was back to his old self. I swear to God, Proctor, there were tears in his eyes."

"And Taylor?"

"Mr. Blaine loves his children, you know that,

but he isn't a fool. He played the game, then took me out to dinner."

"What about Alicia?"

"I didn't see her." Her long, light brown hair began to dance with the strengthening breeze, and she pressed a hand over one ear to keep some of it in place, to keep the ear covered. "My guess is, she'll stay at the office all day, in her room all night, then show up one day as if nothing had happened."

"You know," he said, moving toward the door, "I've never met her."

"Count yourself lucky. There are," she said, following, "barracuda that would kill to know what she does."

"Strong words."

"I could use stronger if you want."

He opened the door and gestured her in ahead of him. As soon as she stepped inside, Taz said, "Lana has made reservations for dinner tonight. For all of us. She says it's so Franklin Blaine will have a heart attack when he sees the first bill in months from us."

Vivian laughed. Not because Taz looked so earnest, but because he had no idea how close to the truth he was.

"And you," he added, pointing, "are the guest of honor."

"No," she protested quickly. "No."

"Yes," Proctor whispered behind her. It wasn't an argument.

She would have argued anyway, but she didn't want to spoil the mood. She had no idea how truly heavy the tension had been in this house until she had been able to relieve it. It was as if they had all been swimming underwater, and had finally come up for air.

"All right," she agreed. And grinned. "I'll gladly sacrifice my modesty as long as it pisses Franklin off."

Another whisper: "Thank you."

But when she turned around, he was gone, back on the deck, looking up at the sky. How the hell does he do that? she thought, and took a step back when the crow returned to the railing. They both faced the river. She looked from his dark shirt to its dark feathers, and took another step back.

"Weird, isn't it," Taz said quietly over her left shoulder.

The bird flew off again, leaving Proctor alone, a shadow in fading sunlight.

Weird, she answered silently, doesn't begin to describe it.

He paced the length of the deck, glancing through the windows of his living quarters without seeing a thing. As pleased as he was that Vivian's efforts had finally succeeded, he could not help a wish that he had been the one. He could not help feeling a little jealous.

Unreasonable, to be sure, considering the stakes involved, but understandable as well.

Which did not make it any easier.

The deck stopped where the house met the garage, and he looked down just as a squirrel darted out from beneath the redwood.

"Pest," he said.

The squirrel didn't care. An impudent twitch of its tail and it was gone across the grass, caught halfway to the trees by its mate, resulting in a loud tumbling, racing game he turned his back on when he heard Lana call his name.

She stood by the chairs, would not approach where he lived even on the outside. A hand to tell her he was coming, and he took a few seconds to scold himself, to remind himself that Blaine was finally back and, in the end, that was all that mattered.

Nevertheless . . .

"Oh, for God's sake," he said, slapped a stinging palm against his leg, and headed back.

"You know a guy named Garber Kranz?" she said before he reached her.

"No, I don't think so."

She turned to the door. "I've got a fax from him, it just came in. He claims to know your father. Georgia someplace?"

He snapped his fingers as they went inside.

"Damn. Yes, of course I know him. He sent some referrals our way a while back."

"Yours or ours," she asked, obviously not remembering.

"Mine," he answered. "I took one, passed on the others. Let me see it, okay?"

On the wall opposite the glass-fronted bookcase was a series of uneven shelves that housed magazines, some books, his stereo equipment and television set.

Eriko and Taz were on the couch, Vivian and RJ in the armchairs, all watching a movie.

Lana lowered her voice. "Are you sure?"

He nodded, brushed a finger across her shoulder to reassure her. He knew she feared he had been snakebit after what happened to Doc, and it had been true. For a while. For a while he didn't want to know about any pleas or requests for his help; every time he saw one of those letters, he felt ice form in his gut, bile in his throat.

"Go get it, okay?" he said. "Really."

One last doubtful look, and she left the room, giving him time to take his place in the wingback and applaud the choice of film someone had made.

When Lana returned she took one look at the screen, and said, "Good Lord, you're kidding, right? In the middle of the day—a workday, may

I remind certain people in this room—you're watching this stuff?"

"Celebrating, remember?" Taz said.

Proctor pointed. "This," he explained seriously, "is a classic of contemporary cinema, Lana. Christopher Lee. Peter Cushing. Hammer Films. *The Mummy*. Nineteen fifty-nine." He shook his head at her shameful ignorance. "A classic."

"Absolutely," Eriko added enthusiastically. "See, Kharis, he's the mummy, he's the third of the Great Monster Triangle." She held up a finger for each: "The Vampire. The Mummy. The Werewolf."

Proctor, surprised, applauded soundlessly, and grinned when he thought he spotted a blush on her cheeks.

Lana, however, only sighed and handed him a sheet of paper. "Funny she should mention that."

*Proctor, I know it's been a while, but I think I have something for you.*

*We've had some awful stuff going on down here, I'm sending along some things I got from the local paper, but the point of it is, it looks to me like we got ourselves some nut who thinks he's a damn wolfman. I wouldn't bother you normally, this being not as weird as the things you like, if I remember correctly, but there's what they call the extenuating circumstances. One of the missing ladies looks a lot like some-*

*one in that picture you sent down late last year, the one called Maude Tackett, except down here she goes by the name of Maudie Batts. Didn't notice it then. She's one of them New Age ladies who claims she's some kind of witch. Looks like she must have run out of spells.*

*The thing is, Proctor, I could sure use your help.*

*I think that thing's after me, whatever it is.*

He didn't realize they had switched the television off until he looked up and saw them watching him.

Maude Tackett.

"Vivian, do we still have use of Taylor's plane?"

She nodded.

"Taz . . ." He hesitated as he passed the fax to him. The young man had been in the thick of the Atlantic City investigation, had nearly been killed himself by what they had ended up hunting. He was resilient, but Proctor wasn't sure how far that resilience would stretch before snapping. Maybe he ought to wait for Murray.

Maude Tackett. One of the two girls who had vanished along with Celeste Blaine.

But Taz, after reading the message himself, handed it to Vivian, and said, "When do we leave?"

# SEVEN

Proctor had been on Blaine's private jet twice, and knew that if he had his way he would never fly commercial again. The dozen seats were armchair large and soft leather, spaced carefully throughout the large cabin for maximum comfort, and privacy if needed. They could be unlocked at the base if necessary and swiveled so conversations could be held without contortions. There was a full galley in back, a shower, even a small bedroom.

With Taz and Vivian opposite and facing him, he sat by a window, the stiff shade up, but there was nothing to see. The landscape was buried by a rumpled cover of clouds. Silent rain streaked the window. The plane juddered now and then. The lighting had been dialed down, which made the inside more comfortable, and the outside darker.

"Maybe we should have driven," Taz said, checking the window in case the view had changed, then glanced at Vivian, who appeared to be dozing. "The train. Don't they have those high-speed trains now?" He shook his head, smiled broadly, falsely. "Bullet trains, right? That's what they call them, I think. Bullet trains."

The plane shimmied.

Proctor watched the grey; it didn't look as if they were moving.

Vivian turned her head and opened one eye. "Pretend it's a highway. You're just feeling bumps in the road."

"Damn big bumps," he muttered, and she laughed silently, poked him with an elbow.

"We won't be long, don't worry."

Proctor smiled. Taz could stand on the point of the roof, stand on the edge of the Palisades, climb nearly to the top of one of the Douglas firs at home, all without a problem. Airplanes, however, were another story entirely.

The plane dropped sharply a few feet and something rattled in back.

Before leaving Newark Airport that morning, Blaine's pilot had informed them that the weather ahead might complicate the flight plan, and it would probably take longer to reach Alton, Georgia, than he had anticipated. He saw no reason, however, to delay their takeoff more than a few minutes.

Taz had been just fine until they'd flown into the clouds.

"You know," Taz began, and Proctor hushed him with a look.

The engines whined; they had begun their descent.

Once Black Oak had absorbed all the data from all the previous investigations private and official into Celeste's disappearance, Proctor had attempted to contact people who had known her and her friends. Ginger Hong's family absolutely refused to talk with him or anyone else associated with Taylor Blaine. Embittered by the diminishing lack of cooperation of the police over the years, and stung by Blaine's seeming disinterest in anyone but his own daughter, they had closed the case on their own child a long time ago. Ginger was lost to them forever. Reminders were unnecessary, and forbidden.

But Miriam Tackett had, in January, agreed to a meeting. Because Proctor would be in England at the time, Doc had suggested Taz be involved because, he had explained, he's a good talker when he has to be, he's brighter than some people give him credit for because he's so good-looking, and with those looks he can charm any woman alive into telling him things they might not tell anyone else. He's a man in boy's clothes, Proctor. The girl's mother will trust him.

Vivian had gone along for moral support, and to protect Taz from whoever it was who wanted the investigation ended.

She had also cautioned Proctor of the delicacy of the trip. "Her husband . . ." She had scowled, looked away, disgusted. "He left a couple of years ago. Thinks she's obsessed and refuses to admit that their daughter is probably dead." The scowl had faded into sadness. "I hope we don't raise her hopes."

As it turned out, Maude's mother had little hope left. Yet neither had she surrendered as completely as her husband had done. She spent several hours talking with them—mostly to Taz, as Doc had predicted—creating a portrait of her only child as a girl soon to be a woman, intrigued by her future, increasingly interested in spiritual matters, fascinated by the potential promised outside organized religion. The New Age had captured her imagination. And, her mother had supposed, that of her friends as well.

The plane dropped. Hard.

"*Son . . . of a bitch,*" Taz yelped.

"Kranz claims this Batts woman calls herself a New Age witch," Proctor said. "And there's a physical resemblance. I don't know how clear, but he claims it's there."

"So," Vivian said, "what do you think?"

"When we see her," he answered. "Not before."

"When we find her," she corrected.

"Yes. When we find her."

From the public address system the pilot asked

them to prepare for landing, his voice not altering pitch a bit when the jet swerved sharply to the left as if punched by a fist of wind. Taz rotated his seat immediately and hastily locked it in place. Vivian was more casual, but Proctor noticed she was a little more pale, the spray of light freckles across her cheeks a little darker.

The plane dropped again; the engines worked hard and loudly.

Proctor adjusted his seat belt and returned his attention to the window, watching the clouds thin and shred until, abruptly, he could see the ground, not all that far away. Farms, white houses, brick houses, and what tree-lined roads he saw were no wider than two lanes.

There was no rain, just racing cloud cover, daylight bright even without the sun.

If you're down here, Maude, he thought; if you're here, why? What have you been doing for the past thirteen years?

Immediately the runway appeared under them, the jet dropped onto it, no run-up time, and the engines screamed in reverse. He noted two hangars, a cluster of small private planes, and a low single-story whitewashed building he assumed was the terminal. There were no jetways —they'd have to walk from wherever they parked.

And as soon as they slowed to taxiing speed, Taz said, "Screw it, I'm walking back."

*    *    *

Police Officer Bobby Grace stood in the departure/arrival area and watched the sleek jet taxi off the runway. He liked working the airport, loved watching the planes take off and land, watching who was leaving, who was arriving. Sometimes he actually got to see famous people, like the time he actually stood next to Johnny Cash or, that other time, when he helped carry Chet Atkins's bags to a waiting limousine. Most of the time, though, it was just businessmen coming in, and folks like the mayor, who had to travel to Atlanta once in a while to remind the politicians up there that Alton and Burline County still existed.

Lately, he figured it would be good just to keep track.

When there was nothing doing, he would flirt a little with Erlene Hotchkiss at the sandwich concession, the food being good enough that people often came here just to have lunch, sit in the plastic seats, and watch the planes, read the paper, watch the weather. The wall behind him had no glass at all, half of it fronted by a single long counter divided in food, ticket, and information sections. The people who worked there, like Erlene, often did double duty—flipping a burger while selling a newspaper, selling a ticket while calling around to see who had room in one of the local motels.

Bobby sighed contentedly. He had already done his flirting today and sometimes, like today, Erlene actually flirted back, although, being a cop, he figured that with his luck it was more likely the uniform, not him. Despite his age—six weeks this side of twenty-seven—he had a touch too much around the waist, and his tight curly hair had given him unfortunate nicknames over the years, the kindest of which had been Brillo.

He didn't care, though; not anymore.

He was special now, a cop, so he would flirt, eat, make his rounds, and reluctantly return to his patrol car for the rest of his tour.

Today, however, he had heard talk among the counter folk that flights were having a time getting in, what with the wind and all. He decided to stick around. If there was an accident, he wanted to be in a position to lend a hand. A quick, sly grin. Good ol' Bobby Grace, they'd say. Hell of a guy, y'know? Man's a damn saint.

The dumb shits, he thought, and he almost laughed aloud.

"Hey," a soft voice said beside him.

He smiled easily. "Hey."

Although he was average height, Erlene was still a head shorter. A little pudgy, her dark red hair trapped in a hairnet that glittered under the recessed lights, her grey-and-maroon uniform maybe too snug for some of the old ladies in town, but definitely not too snug for him.

She lifted a chin toward the jet. "Who's that?"

"Don't know. Just got in. Why, you hear something?"

"Nope. Just wondering."

A lot of people were "just wondering" these days. Rumors had sprung up like weeds—the FBI was sending special agents down to search for the serial killer; the CIA wanted to find the werewolf and trap and train it; Hollywood producers were about to swoop down and sign everybody in sight to contracts so, when the killer was caught, the movies could be made in a hurry.

Curious rumors to have when none of this had yet made the national news and, if Mayor Posten had anything to say about it, never would, either.

"You hear about Royal Blondell?" Erlene asked as the jet maneuvered into the broad tarmac parking area and stopped.

"Erlene, 'course I heard about him."

Her hand brushed his arm. "Never been one right in town before."

"I know. Kind of gets to you, don't it."

Like, he thought, I actually care about that jerk. No loss to the world, that's for damn sure.

A door opened in the fuselage and a man in uniform unfolded the steps.

Bobby's breath hitched when the first passenger out was a woman, one hand to the side of her head trying to protect her hair from the wind as she climbed down. She wore a tan ladies' suit jacket and matching pants, a white shirt, and those shoes that don't have any heels, that look like ballet slippers, or those things Chinese people wear in the kung fu movies he liked.

Lord, he thought; if she ain't a movie star, there's no justice in the world.

Two men were behind her, but he ignored them, following the woman's progress across the tarmac, watching the way she moved, so light on her feet. It reminded him of—

"Bobby Grace, did you hear one word I said?" Erlene scolded, slapping his arm playfully.

He jumped, and grinned his embarrassment. "Sorry, Erlene," and turned away from the window.

"I was saying, I wonder why it was in Mr. Kranz's house. That's kind of spooky, don't you think?"

He knew what she meant. They had both had Mr. Kranz in high school, and while he was a pretty nice guy, fair and all, there was always something a little off about him. Always wanting to dig up old things and read them like they was books, just like Blondell. Now he was gone and Blondell was dead in the teacher's doorway.

"Well, I'll tell you," he began, and said nothing more as the trio from the plane entered the building. He sensed right away this wasn't an ordinary visit. Usually, days like this, people came in laughing or complaining about the wind . . . talking anyway. Not these three. They walked three abreast right toward him, and there was no question which of them was in charge—the guy in the middle, in the dark shirt and jeans, small bag in one hand, a windbreaker in the other. It was the way he walked, the way he looked right at him.

For no reason Bobby could think of, he almost came to attention.

He didn't like that one bit.

The man in the middle didn't smile, but there was a polite smile in his voice nonetheless: "Good afternoon, Officer. I wonder if you could help us."

"Do what I can, sir," Bobby answered, using his best formal-friendly tone.

"We need to rent a car, find a place to stay, and we need to find the address for someone we're here to see. If you can't help with that last one, maybe you can tell me where I can get a local map."

"That's easy," Erlene answered before Bobby could open his mouth. She pointed toward the pair of double doors at the far end of the building. "See down there, the part of the counter with the big red sign? You talk to Dee, she can get you anything you want. Real cheap, too. And," she added, making no bones about taking in that young guy with all the hair, "if you're hungry, you can grab something over there," and she pointed again, to her counter. "Best hot dogs in town."

Jesus, Erlene, Bobby thought; jump him right here, why don't you?

"Who are you looking for, sir?" he said, taking a half step forward. "Do my best to give you the right directions."

"Kranz," the man said. "I'm looking for a man named Garber Kranz."

Proctor said nothing when the cop turned to his lady friend, and said, "Erlene, why don't you scoot on back to work, okay? I'll talk with you later."

She didn't argue, didn't smile. She made an almost military about-face and hurried away, her shoes' soft heels squeaking against the polished floor. He expected her to look back at least once, but she didn't.

"Sir, do you mind if I ask why you're looking for Mr. Kranz?"

Proctor shifted his windbreaker from his hand to over his shoulder. "It's business"—a glance at the maroon name tag on his breast pocket—"Officer Grace."

The cop looked pointedly at the jet still parked outside the terminal. "If you don't mind me saying so, it's a heck of a fancy way to visit a high school teacher."

Proctor gave him a one-shoulder shrug and kept silent.

Grace tapped a finger thoughtfully against his utility belt, then drew it across a blond mustache still new enough to be nearly invisible. He sniffed once, and shrugged back, smiled as his tone lightened. "So, are you all friends of his?"

Going from police officer stiff to good-ol'-country-boy friendly so abruptly and blatantly was enough for Proctor to decide that he had had it. His stomach was slightly queasy from those last few minutes of the flight, and a headache had taken root right between his eyes. What he wanted was a little help; what he had gotten was a conversation that had turned none too subtly into an interrogation. So, with a quick smile of his own that was neither apology nor a dare, he said, "Well, Officer Grace, thanks for your help," and walked away, Taz and Vivian behind him.

He hadn't gone more than a few yards before he heard Grace say, "Sir, hang on a minute," less a request than a command.

"Get the newspapers and a car," he told Taz, turned, and waited patiently until the cop was forced to come to him. Although the approach was meant to be military smart and carefully intimidating, Proctor saw the inexperience, and a slight case of nerves.

"Officer," he said calmly before Grace could speak, "we've had a hell of a flight, we're tired and a little shaky, and we'd like to get settled in. So unless we've broken some kind of law or regulation, what do you say we do this some other time."

He watched Grace consider it, and the consequences of not doing whatever it was he was doing, and when at last he nodded, Proctor said, "Thanks," and walked away again.

The others waited for him at the exit, Vivian tossing him a set of car keys when he reached them.

"What was that all about?" she wanted to know.

"I have no idea," he answered.

"Guess again," Taz told him, and showed him the front page of the local paper. "We haven't even been here ten minutes, and it's already hit the fan."

# EIGHT

Deke Spangler sat on an old rickety folding chair outside his body shop office. His big hands were splayed over his thighs, his legs stretched straight out, and a stained baseball cap was pulled low over his eyes. On his left was a cooler filled with ice and beer; on his right, the empty cans neatly stacked. The worst part of it was, he didn't feel a damn thing, although he didn't think he'd ever felt so lousy in his life. Not only was old Royal dead, Deke had been the one to break the news to Polly Dove.

She lived alone in an old place not far from Kranz's house, and he'd caught her first thing this morning, just as she'd walked out the front door.

He had been at the foot of the walk, and something about him, he guessed, told her how bad it was before he had even opened his mouth.

"No," she'd whispered, dropping her purse, shaking her head. "He had a burger yesterday,

Deke. You saw him. You were there. He had a burger. I made it just like he likes it."

He had picked up the purse and she'd snatched it away, held it tight against her scrawny chest. A swallow, and she set her jaw, stared right at him.

"Tell me."

He did.

The look on her face just about killed him right there. If she had cried, or even fainted, that would have been okay, a natural reaction. But she hadn't. She had just stared at him as if he were a stranger, reached out to pluck something from his coveralls, took a long deep breath, and said, "You find the goddamn bastard that did this, Deke. You find that son of a bitch and you bring me his heart." Then she had walked away, back into the house, the door closing so slowly, so quietly, he winced as if she had slammed it.

An eighteen-wheeler growled past, kicking up pebbles, setting a dust devil in motion in its wake.

He raised his head, looked at the sky, thanked God it was so damn gloomy today. He didn't think he could stand it if the sun was out, making even his shop look halfway decent.

He said something to the traffic that sped by his place, but he didn't know what it was. Probably a curse, except he thought he was pretty much all cursed out.

It wasn't a prayer.

He reached for another beer.

Maybe it was a wish. Maybe he was wishing he hadn't heard such awful news from someone like Bobby Grace. Deke had been over at the police station first thing that morning, examining a nasty dent in one of the patrol cars, doing estimates in his head, figuring how to make a profit without losing the account. Grace had come out back, all strutting and marching like he always did, that uniform so sharply creased it was a wonder he didn't cut his legs off when he sat down.

Bobby had never liked Royal, hated the attention Royal got in those magazines and things. "Uneducated man's got no right to that," he had complained once, and it was all Deke could do to keep from popping him one. So while he was proper sad and all, handing out the awful news while making sure Deke knew the grisly details, Deke could see the pleasure he got from spreading the misery.

He checked his watch—a couple of hours to sundown—and decided, what the hell, one more beer and I'll get the old shotgun, see what I can find, 'cause Mr. Officer Robert E. L. Grace couldn't find his ass with both hands and a map.

The tannic water surged, bubbles rising to the surface, spreading out, sliding under the knees of gnarled cypress. Two eyes and a long snout broke the surface, drifted, and sank again. An island of dead leaves floated with a current that hardly seemed to move at all. Mist in long streams hovered over the water. A cottonmouth glided out of the water, through a spiky hillock, and into the water again, without a sound. An alligator coughed. Sunlight in the Lakochebala was so filled with motes it looked like mottled fog.

In a two-story shack at the edge of an island as much mud as dry earth a gas lantern glowed in one of the front windows; the rest were dark. The porch roof sagged at one end, the vines around the corner post working patiently to pull it down. A short dock poked unsteadily into the water, its uneven planks grey and gaping; tied to it was a crude dugout, a paddle resting at the stern.

Wood creaked.

A bird called.

From inside the shack the sound of someone humming:

*in the Pines*
*in the Pines*


The kitchen smelled of lemon cleaner, and every surface looked smooth as ice. No dishes in the sink, no lingering trash in the step-open garbage pail, a hand towel folded neatly through the refrigerator door handle, a dishrag folded neatly over the faucet.

There were water stains on the ceiling, and the linoleum had begun to wear through its color, but it was a place where, like Polly's momma used to say, you could eat off the floor.

Gospel music played softly from the clock radio on the counter. In the yard that backed onto hers, four or five children played at the tops of their voices. The telephone rang several times before giving up.

Polly sat at the table, her back rigid, her hands working her daddy's old .44. She had already cleaned it. Now she dry-fired it, over and over and over again. Swaying back and forth, sometimes side to side, whispering, "Bring me his heart, Deke, bring me his heart."

Alton's town square was, like others around the state, the county centerpiece, not only of justice, but of civic pride. It was quartered by two tree-lined, bench-lined paths at whose intersection was a scallop-rim fountain. In the middle of the fountain, raised on a marble column above the three plumes of water, was a bronze statue of a young man in a tattered Confederate uniform, holding his company standard high while he leaned on the shoulder of a much shorter drummer boy who looked older than Time.

The northwest and southeast sectors were taken up by lawn and gardens; on the northeast was the post office, a utilitarian brick square built two years ago when the old one burned down; on the southwest, facing the corner, was the town hall, marble and granite, columns, a sharp roof with a white bell tower in the center, and atop the tower a weather vane that hadn't turned in the right direction since the end of the Great Depression.

Richard Posten leaned casually against a fluted column and took his time lighting a cigar. He was short, portly, white fringe for hair, and seldom seen without his white suit and a brocade vest. He knew he was a stereotype of an Old South mayor—a glad-hand and a braying laugh, lazy Southern aphorisms and bourbon and branch water. It couldn't be helped, not if he wanted to stay mayor. And he did. Badly. His retirement fund depended on it.

He drew on the cigar, examined the tip, and said to the man beside him, "Chief, we know who did it yet?"

Police Chief Arthur Macbain shook his head. "Not a clue, Mr. Mayor. To tell you the truth, I don't think it's a man. I mean, I don't think it's human."

"Good God, Art, don't tell me you're believing them werewolf stories."

"No, of course not. I think it's an animal. Don't ask, I don't know, but I don't see any other reasonable answer."

Physically, the only difference between the two

men was the color of their suits—Macbain preferred light tan or cream; and the color of their
skin—he was one of the first Burline blacks to
leave the county and finish college. He did some
cop time in Detroit and Gary, decided he couldn't
stand the winters up there anymore, and came
home with the express purpose of tormenting the
whites who had busted his ass when he was a
kid.

He and the mayor got along just fine.

"This is bad business, Art. Reporters are gonna
start swarming any day now."

"We can handle it."

"Do better, Art, do better. Arrest somebody,
make us look good."

"Give me more money, I'll hire more detectives."

Posten snorted a laugh. "Christ, you people
are all alike, always after money."

Macbain said nothing.

"Oh, Jesus, Art, lighten up. It was a joke."

"Brother Durban was no joke, Richard. I'm
doing the best I can."

"Not good enough."

"Then get a miracle."

"Art, John Verlin's folks are big supporters. We
don't find out who tore their boy up like that, and
damn quick, we're both gonna be out on our
asses." He checked the cigar, glowered at the fine

mist that began to seep from the clouds. "So you're telling me you don't have a thing?"

"Rumors, Richard, just rumors."

"Like? And don't give me no more of that werewolf crap. That's the last thing I need around here, people putting garlic on their doors and stuff."

"That's vampires."

"Who gives a shit."

Macbain drew a thoughtful thumb across his double chins. "You know, it could be Kranz. He's been gone a few days, didn't even leave word at the school he was going anywhere like he usually does. I know he just tutors kids since he retired, but he's pissed them off pretty good over there this time."

"That queer?" The mayor spat over the railing. "Come on, Art, give me something else, huh? Something good. And soon, Art. Give it to me soon."

He returned inside without waiting for a response. Push came to shove, it would be Macbain's neck, not his, that would stretch when voters decided to howl for a scapegoat. But he was next in line, and he had no intention of being a sacrifice just because some nutcase liked to slice people up.

If Art didn't find somebody soon, then by God, Richard Posten would.

\* \* \*

The lamp in the swamp shack had been extinguished, the half-rotted shutters closed over the windows.

The dugout was gone.

Bits of sunlight sparkled on the water, and through the leaves there was the first sign of the rising moon. Pale, but growing stronger.

On the western edge of the swamp, Sissy Brock's sixteen-year-old brother, Cooper, sat in his old man's pickup, his birthday present pump shotgun across the passenger seat. The cops had already been through, but except for Bobby Grace, none of them knew this area, or the swamp, the way Cooper did. And Grace was a prize asshole, so that took care of that.

What Cooper was thinking, and it was something no one else had even considered, was that it could easily be a gator that had done all the killing. They sure chomped like hell; they could outrun a man from a standing start for thirty yards or so; and it didn't take a whole lot to piss them off. Get one big enough, angry enough, and crazy enough, and you got the perfect murder machine.

So in the truck's bed he had a canoe and paddles; at hand was the shotgun, and in back was a halogen handlight. Not to mention the big silver crucifix he wore around his neck. Just in case. Come sunset he would be on the water, sticking close to shore. He didn't care how long it took. If it was all week, that was all right, as long as he came back with the animal that took his only sister.

They laughed at her, she knew, the old lady who lived on the road that followed the north rim of the Lakochebala. She had long since stopped caring. Her house, unlike the way it was described in campfire stories kids told in the autumn, was small and neat and paid for. And unlike the gossips told it, she was anything but poor; wearing old clothes that hardly matched was her choice because she seldom bothered to go any farther than her front porch. She never socialized, never gave teas, so why spend money on dresses she didn't like and no one ever saw?

She was a tall woman, hunched and much thinner than her billowing dresses implied. Her fingers were long and mostly bone, the skin of her neck taut and hard; little flesh remained over once full cheeks, and what flesh there was had been darkened by the sun; white hair and pink scalp; one eye milky, the other fading blue.

They laughed at her, she knew, because most of them were afraid.

Beyond the laughter were whispers: She talked funny because she was from the other side of the world, forced to leave her home because they were going to burn her at the stake; she used to be a movie star in the old days, but they don't want her anymore; she dances naked with the Devil; she can see into your soul.

Whispers: She *knew* things, she could *do* things; animals talked to her, the weather obeyed her, and there were jugs and jars in that house filled with potions and powders and unspeakable things.

Most of it was exaggerated; not all of it was wrong.

Her name was Riza Noscu, and tonight she was afraid.

# NINE

"You know," Taz said, looking out the motel-room window, "I hate that drizzly, misty kind of rain. I really hate it."

"Really," said Proctor.

"No kidding."

"Why?"

"Because it feels like spiders crawling all over my face, creeping in my hair."

Their room at the Southview Inn was motel basic—two beds with a nightstand between them, a long and low dresser with a swivel-stand TV bolted to one end, wall mirror in the center, lamp on the other end. A desk and chair. A small round table and matching chair at the window. An armchair between the table and the nearest bed.

At his request they were on the top, second floor, happenstance putting their room and Vivian's directly over the main entrance so they could see most of the road that led into Alton, and the shrub-lined drive that curved up to the Inn. Across the highway was a large cotton field and what looked like woodland beyond it. On this side the Inn was flanked by unused, overgrown fields—one had a deserted and dying farmhouse and partially collapsed barn, the other held no sign of a habitation at all.

Taz, his shirt off and a towel draped around his neck, his hair still damp from a recent shower, made a face at the weather, refocused and looked at Proctor's pale reflection. "How are you feeling?"

"Better."

The headache had grown rapidly, shooting sparks behind his eyes. He had never had anything like it before, wondered if this was what a migraine felt like. If it was, he didn't know why people who had them didn't just blow their heads off to end the agony. As soon as they reached the Inn, suggested by Erlene's friend at the car rental counter, he had stumbled into the room, pulled the drapes, swallowed a bunch of aspirin and fell onto the bed.

For the longest while he listened to Vivian and Taz moving around quietly, their whispers fading into the sound of sawgrass hissing on a dune, the sound of sand hissing across sand.

When the sound stopped, he opened his eyes and found himself on the redwood deck outside his bedroom. The night was warm, and despite the New York light across the Hudson, there were more stars in the sky than he'd ever seen before.

The moon was full and too big, a western moon that should have been over a desert.

Something bothered him but he couldn't remember what. He scratched through his hair, scratched his chest, yawned so wide he nearly split the corners of his mouth. Something . . . he had been, he thought, working out something important in his dreams, but for the life of him, now, he couldn't remember what it was, although he knew it was something he needed to know.

When he felt someone touch his arm, he stiffened, but he didn't turn.

*Hello, Proctor.*

He sighed.

It was her voice, and that's when he knew he had to be dreaming, because she had left him in Atlantic City, slipping into the night in a dark green dress woven through with hints of silver.

*Hello, Petra.*

*You're in trouble again.*

He smiled. *Looks that way, Or about to be, anyway.*

Her accent faintly European, her voice soft as the last kiss she had given him. *I can help you, but only a little.*

*Thanks, but I don't even know what the problem is yet.*

*Yes, you do. You haven't even given it a second thought. You accepted without question.*

He supposed that was true, but he always left room for doubt. He had to. Doubt, in a strange way all these years, had kept him alive.

*I give you a name,* she said, standing beside him, taking his left hand in hers. *You will not remember it, but you will know it when you hear it.*

He still hadn't looked at her.

He didn't have to.

*Very mysterious.*

*Her name is Noscu.*

*And she is . . . ?*

She leaned her head briefly against his arm. *You will find out.*

*And this woman . . . she's important?*

Her voice grew urgent, somber. *Listen to her, Proctor, listen. If you don't, my dear, you are all going to die.*

He did look then, and before he could react she leaned close and up and kissed him so lightly it made him dizzy.

When it was done, he said, *Petra, are you here? I mean, are you really here or is this—*

A finger against his lips. *You know the old saying, Proctor. Ask me no questions, I'll tell you no lies.*

She walked away then, soundlessly up the deck, untouched by the moon.

He watched until he could see her no more, looked up and watched the stars fade, the moon shrink, the night deepen. He closed his eyes to keep the touch of her, the smell of her, the sense of her with him. Smiling as he had seldom smiled for anyone before.

When he opened his eyes, Taz had grinned, and said, "Has anyone ever told you that you sleep like the dead?"

He took his time in the shower, shaking off the bits of sleep that clung stubbornly enough to prevent him from thinking straight. There had been a dream, he remembered that much, but he had no idea what it had been about until he stood at the basin and began to wipe the shower's condensation off the mirror with a hand towel. Droplets were left behind that distorted the reflection, and for a second he could have sworn he'd seen Petra Haslic standing behind him.

He didn't turn.

Wonderful, Proctor, he thought; now you're dreaming about her. While you're awake, no less.

It had been quite a while, dreaming about a woman, and he wasn't sure how to explain it, how to take it. He had spent a long time, in and since Atlantic City, trying to decipher her, to figure out who, and what, she was. Extraordinary about covered it, and he thought no more about it when Taz called impatiently, reminding him that the afternoon was practically gone because of him, and didn't he think it was time to get to work?

They sat at the table in his room, all the lights on to fight the gloom outside. The mist had become a drizzle, leaving crawling patterns on the window. The woodland beyond the cotton field had drawn back into fog.

For the fifth time, Taz read the lead story in the *Burline Advocate*, and for the fifth time he said, "This doesn't make sense."

Proctor, sitting back, hands folded across his stomach, kept his voice low, steady. "Tell me why."

"Okay. Easy." Taz tapped the newspaper with a finger. "Some guy, this Blondell, is slaughtered in the doorway of the house that belongs to the guy that got us down here." He held the finger up. "The problem is, down here they think that Kranz has been missing for five or six days, maybe a lot longer. And the way they wrote it here, he's either the killer or a victim, depending. Except we know he's not dead because he faxed us only yesterday."

Proctor waited.

Taz stared at the paper again. "But they don't know that, right? They don't know about the fax."

"Then I guess our first job is to tell them."

Taz stared out the window, shook his head. "If

we tell them why we're here, why Kranz got hold of you and we actually made the trip, they'll think we're nuts."

"Why?"

"The werewolf thing."

"I thought we were here because of Maude Tackett."

The young man looked to Vivian, who only raised her hands in a *keep me out of it* gesture.

"Look, Boss, you can't separate them. At least not now. There's a pretty demented serial killer down here, the woman we're after is missing, and now the guy who wants us is missing, too. Which means if we want to find one we'll probably have to . . . we should . . . okay, wait a minute." He stared at the window. A hand waved over the paper. "This stuff isn't . . . it's . . ."

"Peripheral," Vivian suggested.

"Yeah. Right. That. I mean, this stuff is important and all, but we have to try to find that Tackett woman. Or Batts. Whatever. We have to see if she's really Celeste's friend." He slapped the table, nodded once, sharply. "That's what we have to do."

Proctor watched him preen without actually moving, waiting to see if he would find something to trip over, make him start the process again. When he judged sufficient time had passed, he massaged the back of his neck briefly, and said, "Right. And since Kranz isn't around yet to help us, I think we ought to show Maude's picture to a few people, just to be sure he wasn't imagining things. If he was, no harm done; if he wasn't . . . we take the next step."

"Which is?" Vivian said.

He turned his head slowly. "We find her."

Proctor used an enlarged digitally enhanced detail of a photograph Blaine had given him—the three friends standing in front of Celeste's car, ready for their summer-long trip that would eventually land them at their freshman year at Wellesley. Of the trio, Maude was the most plain, with straight brown hair nearly down to her hips, a nose too large, a mouth too big, hips too wide. She wore an improbable combination of granny dress and concho belt, and a double-strand necklace made of Greek worry stones.

June 1984: the last time anyone had seen the young women.

He tried the desk clerk first, a simple question: "Do you recognize anyone in this picture?"

The clerk did not, and neither did the manager, who came out of his office when he heard. When they asked why he wanted to know, he thanked them and left.

The plan wasn't complicated. Since he'd slept through lunch, he was hungry. Since Maudie Batts had a store near the square, they would find a place to eat there and drop in on her shop-keeper neighbors.

Luck presented them with a parking space outside an Italian restaurant a block from the square. Proctor paused before entering, pleased with what he saw. Large oaks whose branches had been clumsily trimmed were unevenly spaced along the curbs, to make the street appear less formal. The buildings themselves were two or three stories high, seemingly equally divided between wood and brick facades. Offices and apartments above the shops; streetlamps fashioned like nineteenth-century gaslights; no litter, no rush. He had a feeling that, until recently, there wasn't much reason for people to lock their doors.

It was clearly an old town—not all the paint was fresh, there were cracks in the sidewalk, a handful of storefronts were empty, many of the buildings had a tired air about them—but it wasn't dying.

It was, he decided, comfortable.

Finally, he joined the others, well aware that more than a few of the customers in the crowded room had marked his progress from door to table.

"I feel like I have 'damn Yankee' stamped on my forehead," he grumbled as he took his seat.

"Pick," Vivian ordered, handing him a menu. "I'm starving."

Then Taz said to her, "You want me to hang that up?"

She wore a dark brown leather coat that hung to mid-thigh, open now and pushed away from her lap. "No. But thanks."

"Man, you must be hot."

"Not in here."

"I mean, outside."

"I'm used to it."

"Your funeral."

Proctor lowered his head without comment to study the selections. He knew why she wouldn't take the coat off; something else the kid would have to figure out for himself. He had learned the answer months ago, when Blaine had suggested she work with him, travel with him when she could. At first the idea that he needed protection was galling, insulting. Since he had learned what she could do, however, he hadn't raised another complaint, either to Blaine or himself.

Eventually Taz would understand why she walked the way she did—lightly and gliding, why she seemed to know everything that happened around them, why every move she made seemed tantalizingly simple.

She was an expert at what she did.

She wore the coat because she was armed.

\*     \*     \*

The waiter could not identify anyone in the photograph. After the meal was over, Proctor cornered two others, with the same results. He wasn't discouraged. The evening was young and Alton was a lot larger than a single small business.

At the register he placed the photograph on the glass countertop as he signed the credit card slip. "You know any of these people, miss?"

The cashier, a woman he figured to be no more than twenty, squinted at it for a while and finally shook her head. "No, sir, sure don't."

He smiled his thanks, picked up his receipt, but wasn't fast enough to stop a hand from reaching around him to grab the photograph. When he turned sharply, he faced a middle-aged man in white shirtsleeves and red tie, a shadow-beard, and black hair almost as thick as Taz's.

The man tapped the picture against Proctor's chest. "What the hell you think you're doing, bothering my people?"

Proctor stepped aside as an elderly couple came up to pay their bill, and the man stepped with him, keeping the distance between them no more than a foot.

"Who are you?" Proctor asked politely.

The man pointed toward the ceiling. "Ascante. I own the place." He tapped Proctor's chest again. "You didn't answer my question."

Proctor held up his hands in apology. "If I

bothered your employees, sir, I'm sorry." But when he reached for the picture, the man jerked it away.

"Listen, pal, I don't know who the hell you think you are, but I don't want you in my place no more, *capisce*? I got good kids here, I don't need them getting upset by some whatever the hell you are. What, a private eye or something? Working some goddamn sleazy divorce or something?"

Proctor looked over his shoulder at Taz and Vivian. "Wait outside."

"Hey, I'm talking to you," Ascante complained.

This time, when the man tapped his chest again, Proctor grabbed his wrist with his left hand, plucked the photograph away with his right, and leaned close enough so that his lips nearly touched the man's ear . . . smiling for the benefit of the diners looking his way:

"I apologized once. I'm not going to do it again." He tightened his grip when the man tried to pull away. "And do not. Ever. Touch me again."

He released the wrist as he stepped back, giving the man credit for watching his eyes, not the smile.

The man's chest rose, fell, and he blinked rapidly a few times before blowing out a breath. "Hey, I'm sorry, okay? You may not know it, not being from here, we're kind of under the gun these days. Nerves aren't doing so well, if you know what I mean."

Proctor nodded, once. He wanted to call him on the fact that his mild Italian accent had somehow disappeared, instead held up the picture. "Do you recognize anyone?"

The man's mouth opened, shut, and he shook his head in admiration. "Man, you sure got a brass pair, don't you?" He fished wire-rim glasses from his shirt pocket, held the picture close, and said, "Nope, don't . . . hey." A frown. "Hey." He pointed. "Jesus, is that . . . Nah, it can't be. Damn, is that Maudie Batts?"

# TEN

Cooper Brock checked his watch against the dashboard clock and figured he'd cripple himself if he sat there much longer. He hadn't heard a thing in over an hour, and that had been when a family of deer thrashed through the woods. Luckily no one saw him start so violently his head hit the roof. If word got around that some damn deer scared him half to death, he'd have to move to goddamn Texas to get over it.

After making sure he had his pockets stuffed with extra shells, he climbed down from the cab, pulled the shotgun after him, and reached in the back for the halogen lamp. It wasn't all that dark yet, but he switched it on anyway, for a test and to see how the beam, aimed at the leaf-broken sky, looked to go on forever.

The only thing he didn't like about it was that it turned everything a sickly grey.

Satisfied, he thumbed it off and fetched his

baseball cap from the front seat, jammed it on, and closed the door carefully, quietly. When he was sure he had everything, and double sure he had the keys, he tucked the stock under his arm and stepped away from the pickup.

The drizzle had gone on long enough now that water had begun to drip from branches and leaves. Swamp mist curled up over the banks, slipped into the underbrush, gathered in clearings and glowed in the fading light. The smell of rotting leaves and wood intensified. Back toward the white pine woods he heard an owl call. Bullfrogs and peepers—bass and tenors. Something splashed in the swamp, probably a fish going for the gnats that swarmed over the surface.

He touched the crucifix under his shirt for luck, rolled his shoulders, and told himself to get moving. It was a last-minute change in plans—before it got too dark, he wanted to roam for a while. Maybe he could find something the others had missed. He sure hoped so, one way or another, because if he came back with nothing, his old man was gonna whomp his ass from here to Macon and back.

On the other hand, if he was right, he would be a damn hero, and get one hell of a pair of new boots out of what was left of that gator after he'd blown it hell to gone.

He moved cautiously along a deer trail, using the lamp whenever the shadows grew too deep.

Water slithered down the back of his neck.

The mist began to rise into fog.

Every ten or fifteen yards he stopped and listened, cocking his head, concentrating, hearing nothing he hadn't heard before.

Until, as he started back toward the truck, he heard the first howl.

Riza Noscu sat in her kitchen, fading greylight from outside dulling all the years-old colors on the walls. On the table was a saucer containing dried bay leaves; a tiny flame consumed them slowly. Another saucer was half-filled with milk. A third served as a catch for a tall white candle whose flame tried to bob away from the drafts that slipped in around the back door and the room's only window.

Despite the oppression of rain and humidity, she wore a fringed shawl over her shoulders, a kerchief over her head. Her fingers skated over a jumble of colored stones, worn smooth by decades of touch and rub. She did not watch her hands; she watched the back door instead—the inner one was open, the screen door shut. Through it she could see her flower gardens, her herb gardens, gnarled fruit trees whose new leaves and buds promised nothing.

When she heard the first howl, she closed her eyes and trembled.

Deke Spangler sat on the hood on his old Chevy parked on Swampline Road and smoked a cigar, daring the weather to put it out. Across his lap was a shotgun. In his left hand was a can of beer. To his left was a line of heavy trees and thick brush, on the other side of which was the north edge of the Lakochebala. To his right was a cotton field not yet ready to produce. The low plants enabled him to see dark moving objects that made up the traffic on Alton Road. If he squinted, he could just about see the roof of the Southview Inn.

He burped, loudly, and spat onto the road more dirt than blacktop.

Second thoughts had ambushed him on the way there. His driving, he discovered, wasn't all that steady, and it made him wonder if he could even hit a tree if he was leaning against it, much less bring down a moving target.

The only thing that kept him here was his intention to do something to avenge Royal's death.

He coughed harshly, spat, tossed the cigar and the beer can away.

Lots of good times with Royal over the years. Lots of good times. Once, he had even gone with him on one of those expeditions. They hadn't done anything but make a big hole in the ground, but he had developed an increased respect for what Royal did, watching the painstaking routine, amazed at the guy's patience.

Lots of good times.

His head jerked up when he heard the first howl. Couldn't tell the direction, but if he wasn't going to catch the killer, he might feel better if he caught one of them damn feral dogs.

"What do you think, Royal?" he said as he slipped off the hood and danced a couple of clumsy steps to keep from losing his balance. "What do you think?"

He belched hard and loud, so hard and loud he nearly fell over, nearly dropped his weapon.

Ah, screw it.

He staggered to the door, missed the handle the first time, backed away and narrowed his eyes, measuring the distance so he wouldn't miss again. A long step and he slipped, and fell. His head slammed against the door. He yelled. He rolled onto his back. He felt the rain on his face and decided to wait here a while, gather his strength.

His eyes had just closed when the dog howled again.

Closer.

The Reverend Luther Carlton was not unused to hard work in the name of the Lord, but he had never expected anything like this. He crouched in front of Adelia Durban's headstone, stiff brush in one hand, bucket on the ground beside him, and worked at driving the blood from her headstone.

It was hard going, but he refused to give up. The open, empty grave on his left was ready for Brother Spence's coffin as soon as that self-important piece of forgive me Lord shit, Art Macbain, released the body. He did not want Brother Spence's blood, not one trace of it, left here to remind mourners any more than they needed to be of the deacon's unholy demise.

Sweat mingled with the drizzle on his face, and he prayed, not for the first time that day, that the real rain would hurry up and get there, get it over with. For a state that was mired in a vicious two-year drought, it had sure been awfully wet lately. It made it difficult to know exactly what to pray for.

He scrubbed.

He sang soft hymns to himself and Adelia.

And when he heard that first howl, mocking his work, calling for the Devil to ride again, he threw the brush into the bucket and stood.

"That does it," he declared to the graveyard. "Sweet Jesus, that does it."

He grabbed the bucket's handle, apologized to Adelia for not finishing the job, and marched toward his clapboard house on the other side of the clapboard church.

Serial killer, mass murderer, werewolf, were-possum, were-whatever, he was fed up with sitting back while the Devil marched all over his blessed piece of Georgia. It was time for the Lord to get involved, and by Jesus, someone was going to pay.

Cooper froze at the howling, shotgun up and snug under his arm, the lamp darting and flashing through the dusk under the trees. A thick mist-blanket swirled high as his knees, stirred by a cool evening breeze that brought gooseflesh to his arms. The frogs had fallen silent.

He was only sixteen, but he knew that weren't no dog.

Before that retard Royal had been found at Mr. Kranz's place, some of the kids in school had already started making sneak trips to Madam Noscu's place, for charms and whatnot to keep the bad stuff away. Of course, the creeps who lived west of town in the new developments, the big houses with big lawns, they laughed and made fun of the talismans and mojo bags. But when one of their own, Johnny Verlin, was all torn up, they hadn't laughed so hard then.

Cooper planned on sneaking over to Noscu's the next morning, before school.

The next howl sparked him into moving. It sounded closer, but he still couldn't tell the direction. His breathing grew rapid, shallow. Careful strides on the slippery ground became careless as he sped up. The light didn't hold on anything for long, and its jerky swinging motion made the trees charge him and retreat, made his eyes unable to focus right.

The breeze curled around him, much chillier than before.

It didn't take long to realize the lamp was a mistake. Bulky in its plastic case, he couldn't tuck it under his arm to hold the shotgun properly with both hands.

Moving slowly, he crouched and set the lamp on the ground, pumped a shell into the chamber. The noise it made was comforting, and too loud. He took hold of the lamp's thick handle and rose. No sense trying to be quiet now; he wanted to get back to the truck as soon as he could. He wanted out of here.

When he heard a snort behind him, he ran.

He didn't look back.

When his left foot skidded over a patch of wet leaves, he fell and rolled into a thicket, thorns and twigs tearing at his face, his hands, ripping a seam at his shoulder. The lamp rolled in the opposite direction, came to rest facing the way he had come.

Hissing at the stings, made worse by the cold

that passed through him like a ghost, he lurched to his feet, headed over to fetch the lamp . . . and looked back up the trail.

He stopped breathing.

For the longest time, he stopped breathing.

Then, without thinking, he fired from the hip. Pumped, and fired again.

And he ran.

Something—leaf, twig, branch—scraped across his forehead and slapped his hat off, spinning him half-around into a tree whose bark raked his left arm.

He ran.

He didn't think, didn't pray; there was no time for either. He managed to pump in another round and when he found a piece of courage, he turned, trotted backward, and fired into the dark that had swept out of the trees. Turned and ran again, his weapon gaining weight, sweat or blood stinging his eyes, pain like a dull knife making its way around his waist.

There was just light enough to make out the shapes of the growth around him, just light enough for him to realize that he had left the trail. He almost slowed, drove himself onward. If he had been heading for the swamp, he would have reached it by now.

He was in the woods, going deeper, and he was lost.

The crucifix slipped out of his shirt, beat

against his chest until he grabbed it with one hand, and held it tightly when its string broke. The ground rose, and he pelted over a rise, down the other side slipping and sliding but not losing his feet. A minute later, an hour later, he was able to run faster, freer, because he was in the pines.

His face was hot, there was fire in his chest, and when he knew he only had a few steps left in him, he whirled and fired and fell to his knees, lifted the shotgun to his shoulder, and this time he aimed.

He had seen it in the muzzle flash, saw it again when he fired again. He was startled by its coloring—it looked like a fox; but no fox was so big, no fox had that shape.

When it leapt, he swung the shotgun like a bat. The weapon was wrenched out of his hands as the creature snarled past him.

He scrambled to his feet and held the crucifix in his right hand like a knife. Breathing hard, staggering wearily.

It came out of the dark so fast he didn't see it, was driven to the ground before he could react. As he screamed and slashed wildly at the thick pelt, all he could see were those eyes.

And all he could think was: oh, God, I'm only sixteen.

# ELEVEN

Taz stood in the motel room and said, "I don't know why I bothered to take a shower."

A towel flew through the door on his right, landing on his face.

"Rain," Vivian called from her room, "is good for you. It's pure, it's soft—"

"It's cold," he yelled back, vigorously drying his hair. "I'm gonna catch pneumonia, just like my mother warned me."

"Then get a haircut."

He scowled. It was the same thing his mother kept ragging him about. But he liked his long wavy hair. He liked his long lashes. He figured, if his family was any indication, he would eventually end up looking like Doc, so he wanted to hang on to what he had for as long as he could.

As he worked the towel through his hair and over his face, he watched Proctor, who had shoved the table aside and sat at the window. The drizzle was now a full rain, and without lights in the room, shadow-reflections of the storm moved down the man's face.

He didn't move, barely seemed to breathe.

Didn't blink when distant lightning brightened the room for an instant.

"Taz."

He looked across his shoulder. Vivian beckoned with a finger, and he nodded, mimed getting a dry shirt, and did so as quietly at he could.

He knew the boss better than to try to talk to him. He had witnessed these pensive moments before. If he spoke, Proctor would ignore him; if he insisted, Proctor would give him one of *those* looks, the ones that reached inside and pulled out parts of you you didn't know you had. Lana was the only one who could boss him around, and even she wasn't immune when he got like this.

He crossed into the adjoining room, buttoning his dry shirt. She sat at the desk, a gesture over her shoulder telling him to take a chair. In front of her was a small notepad, and he waited patiently as she wrote. That was something he would have to do later too—make his own notes on everything he had done and said and seen tonight.

"So what do you think?" she said without turning around, her voice slightly deep, not quite husky.

He kept his own voice down, as if there were a patient in the next room. "We got six, seven possible hits. I think that's a pretty good sign. Except for those ladies who wanted to know why I wanted to find the Devil's daughter." He laughed. "They don't think much of witches down here, do they."

Vivian placed her pen on the desk and in a motion too smooth and rapid to follow clearly, reversed position in the chair, arms folded over the back, chin resting on her arms.

"You think it's Tackett?"

He nodded. "Yep."

A faint frown at his tone. "You don't like it?"

"Nope."

"Why not? It's what we came for."

He pulled idly at his shirt. Rubbed a finger under his nose. Wished he were back in Jersey, slamming his thumb with a dumb hammer.

"You've been with him," he said. "You know what happens."

"That's not always the case."

"I'm two for two." He shook his head morosely, stared into his lap. "I'm on a streak."

Looking up without lifting his head he saw the smile, mock-scowled at her, and finally grinned, leaned back, cupped his hands behind his head.

"Why can't I get in on the cases where it's the greedy landlord trying to clear a building by pretending its basement has a nest of giant cockroaches?"

"Bad luck."

"Damn right."

The thing about Proctor, aside from the look, was the way he handled things after the fraud had been exposed. Sometimes he called the cops, sometimes the humiliation of exposure was enough, and there were times when all he did was, as he'd once put it, have a quiet word. Whatever that word was, it scared the guy half to death.

Taz had studied the reports; he had talked with Doc.

He knew there were still other times when that *look* and that *voice* translated into something physical. Vivian had seen it, and Taz had long ago decided that was definitely something he could live without.

He shifted as he lowered his arms, tilted his head toward the window. "In case you didn't know, on the other side of that field out there is a swamp."

"Meaning?"

"Sooner or later we're gonna end up in there, fighting mutated mosquitos or wrestling prehistoric alligators or something."

"Don't be silly. How can you know that?"

"Okay, the bugs and the alligators I don't know about. The swamp . . . because it's over there and we are who we are." He lifted a hand. "Fate, Vivian. When we're with Proctor, that swamp is our fate."

She grinned, pushed absently at a fall of hair

over her eyes. Shrugged. "So that has to do with . . . what?"

"There are people missing, right? Maude is one of them. Now that he's sure she's Celeste's friend, only it's fourteen years later, give or take, we're going to have to try to find her."

"He already said that."

But she glanced at the window. Toward the swamp.

Taz didn't mention it. "So that means, one way or another we're going to get involved with this serial killer guy." A loud sigh for her benefit. "And that means you know damn well we're not talking about no serial killer here."

"You're not a psychic, Taz. You can't know that."

He looked at her steadily. "Yes, I can."

"I'm not joking."

"Neither am I."

Before he had a chance to blink, she was up and out of the chair, had it turned around, and was in it again, her legs out, propped on the bed. Her back was to the window.

"That ain't gonna help."

"So you say."

He heard the laugh in her voice, and he stretched, groaned theatrically, and startled himself by sneezing. "Told you," he said, heading for the bathroom to get a tissue. "In and out of air-conditioning all day like this, with the rain, I'm getting pneumonia."

He blew his nose and checked his reflection. It did not look pleased. He gave it a glare and suggested it grow up. For all his bitching and moaning, being at Black Oak definitely beat working at Uncle Carmine's garage. While Carmine spent his life complaining about his cheapskate customers and planning ugly revenge scenarios for the Yankees, Taz got to complain about stuff most people believed only existed in the movies.

On the other hand, none of his uncle's customers ever tried to kill him.

He laughed at himself, shook his head. "Christ, Tazaretti," he whispered, "you're nuts, you know that?"

And he was already on his way before Proctor called his name.

Erlene stood at the foot of the porch steps, shoulders hunched against the rain that thundered on the umbrella she held on to for dear life in both hands. On the road behind her she could hear Dee's car idling and sputtering.

On the porch Madam Noscu watched her discomfort, eyes narrowed, lips working soundlessly. Her hands were at her waist, clasped as if she were holding something delicate that wanted to escape.

"Do you believe, child?" the woman asked.

Erlene nodded rapidly, earnestly, until she remembered Dee telling her that the old witch could tell when you were lying. And when you lied to her, she cursed you.

"I don't know, Madam," she admitted, hating the sound of her little girl voice. "I . . . I want to."

"You are scared."

"Yes, ma'am."

"You want protection."

"Yes, ma'am, I sure do."

The old woman brought her hands to her mouth and blew lightly over her swollen knuckles. "You will make fun of me when you leave?"

Erlene shook her head violently. "Oh, God, no, Madam Noscu. I just don't want to die."

"For this to work, you will have to believe."

"Yes, ma'am, I will, swear to God."

The old woman studied her carefully, her head turning one way, then the other. It reminded Erlene of a bird checking the ground for something to eat. A big bird. A buzzard. That made her shiver, made her bite down on her lower lip. She was sorry now that she'd let Dee talk her into this. It was wrong. It was blasphemy. If she had the courage she'd run right back to the car and scream at Dee to push that accelerator to the floor, let the old witch curse her, she didn't care.

"Come closer, child."

Erlene held her breath, couldn't move.

The old woman smiled at her without showing

any teeth. "Child, I am old. You have the umbrella and I do not. If you want better protection than that, you must come and get it."

Erlene closed her eyes briefly, sucked in her stomach, and moved to the last step. Climbed. Whispered a silent prayer, and climbed to the next one.

"Before I give this to you," Madam Noscu said, "we must talk about payment."

"Oh, I got money, Madam," Erlene assured her. "Not a lot, but I got some, don't worry about that."

"I do not want your money, Erlene Hotchkiss."

Erlene's mouth opened in shock. How . . . how did she know?

The old woman stepped back, beckoned Erlene with a jerk of her head. Erlene took the last step up and lowered the umbrella. She kept her spine stiff, her chin up, thinking that Madam actually didn't look so bad close up. Old as a prophet for sure, but not nearly as scary as when she was seen from a distance.

Madam Noscu reached out a hand, brushed a finger lightly over Erlene's curls. "This is unusual, what you have done."

"It's called a Betty Boop," Erlene told her proudly. "It's supposed to make my face look good." Her voice lowered. "I'm kind of fat, you know. I need all the help I can get."

Madam Noscu smiled again, and shook her

still clasped hands as if she were shaking dice. "You will do a favor for me after I give you this, yes?"

"Whatever you want, Madam," she promised. "I swear, whatever you want."

"You will not cheat me?" Suddenly the old woman scowled. "I will know this if you do. If you cheat me, I will know this."

Erlene crossed her heart, kissed the tips of her fingers. "I swear, Madam."

Slowly, then, the old woman opened her hands, held them out, and Erlene, amazed her hand wasn't shaking off her wrist, picked up the small leather pouch that lay on those callused old palms.

"Around your neck," Madam Noscu instructed, gesturing with a finger. "Never take it off, not even when you bathe. Never open it. Do not shake it. Do nothing, you understand?"

"Yes, Madam, I understand."

She tucked the pouch into her apron pocket, patted it, and tried to smile her thanks.

"The price," the old woman said.

Erlene waited.

When the old woman finished, Erlene blurted, "Is that all?"

"It is more than you think, child, much more. If you fail"—and she pointed at the apron pocket—"not even that will be able to save you." She turned to her door, looked over her crooked shoulder. "Leave. Now. What you fear is already out there. If you stay . . ."

Erlene grabbed her umbrella, ran down the steps and down the walk. At the car she yanked open the door, scrambled inside, and said, "Punch it, Dee. We're going to my place, and we're gonna get drunk."

Someone knocked on the door.

Proctor looked at Taz. "Room service?"

"Don't look at me. I'm not hungry."

"Amazing," he muttered, and pushed away from the table. When he checked the peephole in the door, he stepped back and frowned.

"What?" Vivian said, on her feet immediately.

"Company," was the answer, and he opened the door.

Officer Grace stood in the hall. "Sir," he said, touched a finger to the beak of his uniform cap in a greeting salute, and added, "ma'am."

Proctor tucked a hand into his jeans pocket. "Can I do something for you, Officer? You're working kind of late."

Grace shrugged with one shoulder. "We all are, sir, these days."

Proctor nodded that he understood. "Something we can do for you?"

Grace made sure he had them all in his sight. "Chief Macbain would appreciate it if you would

stop by his office sometime during the day tomorrow?"

"Something the matter? Have we done something wrong?"

"I couldn't really say, sir." A quick apologetic
smile. "I just do what I'm told."

"Well . . . sure. Of course."

"You just go to the square, it's right across the
street from the municipal building. Can't miss it."

A nod, a casual salute, and Grace ambled away.

Proctor straddled the threshold and watched
him moving toward the elevator, left hand in his
trouser pocket. From his attitude he seemed stiff
and tired, and Proctor wasn't surprised. Long
days and killers took a lot out of cops, especially
when they weren't used to it.

He stepped back inside, closed the door, and
locked it.

"What's up?" Taz said, while Vivian settled
herself again.

Proctor didn't answer. He stood at the window
and watched the cruiser swing right into Alton
Road and speed toward town. Then he lifted his
gaze toward the line of trees on the other side of
the cotton field. Rain blurred it all. Lightning
made it vanish.

"Taz?" he said at last, and pointed.

"Cotton, something called Swampline Road,
some trees, and someplace call the Lakochebala
swamp."

He nodded, pressed the pad of his index finger against the pane and felt the chill, the vibration of thunder. The next lightning strike was distant, confined to the clouds, and it turned the droplets on the glass to scurrying darts of silver.

He stepped back.

He had remembered part of the dream.

# TWELVE

As Proctor came out of the bathroom the next morning, Taz pointed at the television. "I think we may be off the hook for a while."

Proctor sat on the edge of the bed and watched as a reporter interviewed a black minister, who was backed by a crowd of supporters holding signs that demanded the police and the mayor do something now to get the Devil out of Burline County.

"Downtown," Taz told him.

Although the crowd shouted slogans and passages from the Bible, the minister answered all the questions passionately but calmly.

When the camera finally swung around to reveal the street in front of the police station blocked by fifty or sixty of the cleric's backers, Proctor said, "Did you see the weather?"

"Sure. Sun, rain."

"Local station?"

Taz nodded.

"Okay. We'll eat downstairs, then see what we can do to find Kranz."

Vivian found the address in the telephone book, Taz got directions from the desk clerk, and after breakfast, they made their way over, Proctor taking his time, trying to get an image of Alton and reconcile it with the brutality that had visited it over the past few weeks.

Not that he expected to succeed.

There was no such creature as the typical setting for either fraud or what most people refused to believe was real. Preconceptions led to complacence; complacence led to the grave.

No one spoke when he finally pulled over; when they left the car, they did it at the same time. No neighborhood dogs or cats, no neighborhood children. Puddles in the middle of the street, miniature ponds where the rain collected in depressions where the gutter would be if there had been any curbs. The clouds had been ripped apart by high-altitude winds, creating huge gaps in the cover, the resulting sunlight blinding outside the shade.

Yellow crime scene tape had been fixed across the still open front door of Kranz's home, and the chewed-up lawn indicated that a great number of people had tramped through there recently. He kicked aside a crushed cigarette pack as he moved up the walk, wondering with a stir of indignation why there wasn't a guard here. Surely, after a crime of such violence, they couldn't have already completed their investigation.

"The backyard," he told Taz, who nodded and moved away.

"They came, they saw, they obliterated any footprints," said Vivian dryly, quietly. "The whole yard should be marked off."

He could see no blood as he approached the stoop; the storm had taken care of that.

He paused on the stoop. According to the paper, Royal Blondell had been found faceup right here in the doorway, most of him in the house, only the soles of his shoes visible from the street. He had opened the door, and he'd been attacked. Proctor hoped it hadn't taken very long.

When he ducked under the crime scene tape, Vivian said, "That's illegal." A comment, nothing more.

In spite of the previous night's wind and the open door, the house felt as if it had been closed up for weeks. His lungs had to work to get a decent breath. And when his vision adjusted, he said, "Jesus."

From where he stood he could see the living room and down a short hall into the kitchen. Almost everything had been destroyed. The furniture had been smashed or torn up, the carpet slashed and pulled away from the flooring. There was little left of the television, and pages from books and magazines stirred like dying fish, though he could feel no breeze. The kitchen table had been overturned, and he could see boxes and broken bottles strewn on the floor. To his right he could see into a bedroom, the mattress ripped and dragged off the bed frame, the frame twisted out of shape. Clothes all over; drawers from a dresser taken apart at the seams.

No wonder there was no guard; there was nothing left here to steal.

"He was a teacher," Vivian said from the stoop. "He must have had an office or a study."

He spotted a doorway in the living room's back wall, its door tilting away from a snapped top hinge and ripped-away frame. He considered crossing over and checking that room as well, then changed his mind. This was more than vicious destruction; he had a feeling this had been a search as well. Kranz, wherever he was now, hadn't been here for a while. If he had anything of importance, it was probably with him or hidden elsewhere.

He rubbed an earlobe between thumb and forefinger, turned around and asked Vivian to leave the stoop and move down the walk a few feet. When she did, he took a step back.

"What do you see?"

"Not much." A wry smile. "You look like a ghost."

He inhaled, took in the stink of soggy carpeting, the acrid stench of short-circuited wiring.

Another breath.

He smelled blood.

He leaned against the car and stared at the house, sunglasses on, hands tucked into his waistband.

There was nothing in the backyard.

"It is possible," he said carefully, "that Mr. Blondell wasn't the one who was supposed to die."

Taz said, "Huh," and shook his head; he didn't get it.

"Vivian stood down the walk a little," he explained, "and I stood just inside the house. She could see me, but not very well." He nodded toward the pecan trees in the yard. "The shade's pretty heavy up there."

"Huh," Taz said again, and Proctor almost smiled.

"When he was killed there was a storm." He pointed down the street. "There's the only streetlight worth talking about, and it sure won't reach this far. No light over the door, either, and all the shades are down. So . . . either someone knocks or rings the bell, or Blondell sees someone coming up to the house. Anyway, he opens the door. The paper said there was a power outage for a couple of hours. It didn't affect the streetlight, but it did affect the house, which is on a different grid."

"So there're no lights on inside. Blondell opens the door, and he's attacked. The house is wrecked. I think it was also searched. Just a feeling, don't ask me why.

"It would have been searched anyway, if Blondell hadn't been here. But he was. So he was killed."

"A little extreme," Vivian said.

"Not if whoever it was thought he was Kranz."

Uncertain what the next move should be and wanting to avoid the downtown square, Proctor kept to the side streets, not driving so slowly that he would attract suspicion, and not so fast that he would attract attention. Before long, Alton proper was left behind, and he cruised on narrow two-lane roads flanked by fields of cotton, cabbage, and what he thought were peanut plants. A few acres of corn. Beef cattle congregated in the shade of wide-crowned trees. Peach orchards. Pecan orchards.

He didn't bother to keep track of time; Taz would let them know when it was time for lunch.

He stopped counting churches when he reached an even dozen.

The temperature was lower than it had been the day before; the broad patches of blue sky had begun to shrink as fresh clouds attracted each other.

Taz said, "I guess he was right, that Kranz guy. He said he thought someone was after him."

Vivian nodded. "So he's either dead already, or he's hiding."

Proctor didn't speak.

"Hiding," she suggested. "The fax, and from the number, it was from another town."

Petra, and *you're all going to die*, was all he could recall of his dream. The failure to remember anything else frustrated him; failure to know if it was a dream at all frustrated him even more.

He would wait until he knew everything before he told the others.

A tap on his shoulder, and he looked to the right, abruptly pulled over onto the mowed verge. A small white building fronted by a crushed-gravel parking lot, sat well back from the road. According to the announcement board by the entrance, it was the Holy Temple of God Chapel, the Reverend Luther Carlton's church.

The man, he thought, on the news that morning.

A low, white picket fence separated the church from a small graveyard. There were no Victorian angels or marble seraphim, no melancholy cherubs or granite crosses. Simple headstones, a rosebush or two, and a large chestnut tree in back whose crown had to be at least thirty feet wide.

Taz said, "They said he emptied a .357 at whoever killed him. He was supposed to be a good shot."

Proctor kept his hands on the steering wheel. "Apparently not."

"But what if he was."

A U-turn headed them back toward town.

Proctor was angry.

A place as peaceful as this, even if it looked worn and tired, did not deserve the slaughter it had suffered.

"Boss?"

"Proctor," Vivian corrected with a smile.

"Yeah. Okay. Proctor."

A few yards into an empty field, two turkey vultures picked at something. A third waddled back and forth nearby, stretching its neck, flaring its wings.

"God, they're ugly," Taz said, making a face that brought a quick laugh from Vivian. He grinned at her. Sobered. "Boss, if there's a werewolf or whatever—and I'm only saying this for the sake of argument—there must be somebody with it, right? I mean, unless they came along a lot later, a werewolf couldn't have searched that guy's house. Right?"

Proctor glanced at the rearview mirror. "Is a wolf always a wolf?"

"A real one? Sure. But—"

"Is a werewolf always a werewolf?"

Taz thought for a moment and then said, "Shit."

* * *

Proctor slowed the car as they approached the motel. Parked near the entrance was a police cruiser, and standing by the driver's door was Bobby Grace. He supposed he could keep on going, but he was in no mood to play games. Even though he understood, and always stressed to his investigators, that their occupation gave them no official status anywhere in the country, he never by suggestion or misdirection pretended otherwise.

"Uh-oh," Taz said when he also spotted the cop.

Proctor turned into the drive. "When I stop, go inside. Do not pass Go. Smile at him, and ignore him if he tells you to stop."

"Asking for trouble," Vivian said.

"We've done nothing wrong."

"Unless somebody saw us at the house."

"I'm the only one who went inside. That's where the tape was, over the door."

He parked by the cruiser, leaving an empty space between them. Vivian and Taz left immediately, with a polite nod, Taz giving him a "How you doing?" Grace did not try to stop them. He leaned back against his vehicle's door and waited for Proctor to get out.

Proctor took his time.

The man had his hat pulled low, his silver-lens sunglasses on. His thumbs were hooked into his belt. By his big smile and greeting nod, his casual stance, a passerby, or someone watching from the motel, would think they were only passing the time of day.

Proctor walked around the car, raised a questioning eyebrow as he leaned back against the passenger door, slipping his hands into his pockets, thumbs out.

He didn't smile.

Grace studied him carefully, tilted his head, shook it in disappointment. "Mr. Proctor, you were supposed to drop in on us, as I recall."

Proctor kept his voice even. "You didn't specify the time."

"I meant this morning."

Proctor shrugged. "I can't read your mind, Officer. All you said was today. When I saw the morning news, I figured your boss had enough on his plate."

Grace's expression didn't change, but he did shift, as if seeking a more comfortable place for his rump. "Well, now, the truth is, Mr. Proctor, you've been disturbing some of our citizens. Upsetting them, in fact."

Proctor stared directly at the silver lenses, as though they weren't there.

The man's tone hardened. "Maudie Batts, maybe she was kind of like her name, but most people like her, Mr. Proctor. They're praying mighty hard she isn't one of the killer's victims.

Then you come along, show this old photo, and they start fretting all over again."

Proctor said nothing.

"The point is, you leave catching criminals to us. You're nothing but an amateur, and all you'll do is cause more trouble."

Proctor almost laughed aloud. "Wait, hold it. Let me get this straight—I show a picture of Maudie Batts to some people, trying to get some information, and you think I'm trying to catch this murderer you've got?"

"If you're not, what are you doing it for?"

The urge to laugh died. "Officer, no offense, but as long as I've broken no laws, that's none of your business."

He was on his way to the motel entrance before Grace had a chance to stop him. He expected a command to stop, but he only felt Grace watching him, deciding his next move. It came when Proctor heard the cruiser's door slam, the engine bellow, and the tires protest as it sped toward the highway.

He hadn't wanted to behave that way, pull civilian rank, but there was something about the young officer that made him wary.

Vivian met him in the lobby, and her expression made him say, "What?"

"There's someone here who wants to talk to you."

He scanned the room, seeing no one but Taz. "What does he want?"

"It's a she, and she wants to talk to you about a witch."

# THIRTEEN

Proctor stood by an armchair, his back to the windows. Because of the furniture and a number of ill-placed and tall potted plants, the room appeared smaller than it actually was. Deliberately so, he thought. The management did not want its customers lingering.

He motioned Taz to join him, put him in a nearby chair without having to say a word. By the time Taz was settled, Vivian was on her way, a short woman at her side Proctor recognized as the sandwich girl from the airport. Bobby Grace's friend. She was still in her uniform, a light cardigan caped around her shoulders. He warned himself to be careful; she looked scared to death.

A smile then as he gestured toward a chair, but she shook her head. "Can't stay," she said, looking nervously toward the front desk. "I'm on my lunch hour, don't want to be late getting back."

"That's okay," Taz said, with a look letting her

know that he knew all about bosses and their lousy rules.

She sidestepped toward him, checked the front desk again. "I don't know how to do this."

Proctor sat, said nothing, and would say nothing as long as Taz was working.

"Nothing to it," the younger man told her. "You talk, we listen. If you have time for questions, that's cool. If you don't, maybe I'll have to come see you later."

Erlene giggled. "My boyfriend would be mad."

Taz made a face, and she giggled again.

"So . . . ?" and he opened a hand in invitation.

She hesitated, her tongue pushing at the inside of one cheek. Then: "Y'all are from up North, right? Things're different down here, you know what I mean? I mean, I don't think we think the same way as you."

Taz nodded; he got it.

She looked to the ceiling for guidance. "All this terrible stuff going on here . . ." She put a hand to her chest. "They say it's one of them serial killers, a crazy guy. You're gonna laugh, but there's some who don't think that. They think maybe it's . . ." She leaned over to whisper. "They think it's a . . . a . . ." She lost her nerve, licked her lips.

"No sweat," Taz told her gently. "I already know the stories." An unspoken promise that he wasn't laughing now and he wouldn't laugh later.

"Okay," she said, nodding quickly. A fearful look at Proctor. "There's this old woman, she's kind of strange. Some say she's a witch and can do weird stuff." Erlene shrugged. "She knows about plants and stuff, though, you know? Swamp willow for a headache, things like that. I, uh . . ."

Proctor saw her eyes begin to redden. She wanted to cry because she did not want to say this, and was afraid not to.

"Erlene," he said, and she blinked at him. "You went to see her."

"Yes, sir, I did. Yesterday."

A half smile. "I'll bet you five bucks it was for a charm."

Amazed, she grinned sheepishly. "Kind of, yes." And her hand returned to her chest.

"She thinks what's going on is a shapeshifter, right?"

The girl frowned, not understanding.

"A werewolf."

Shame that she herself might even consider such a foolish notion made her look down until, softly, he spoke her name again. "Yes, sir," she whispered.

"And you wanted to tell us this . . . why?"

She looked quickly at Taz, who nodded his encouragement. A check of the front desk, a quick check at the parking area she could see through the window, and she took a step closer.

"She wants to see you, Mr. Proctor."

It was Proctor's turn to blink. "I'm sorry, what?"

"She wants to see you. Soon as you can."

"Why?"

"Madam doesn't tell you why," Erlene said, as if he ought to have known that. "She just tells you."

"Erlene, I'm sorry, but I don't know this woman."

"She knows you."

A look to Taz and, over the girl's shoulder, to Vivian. "How?"

"I don't know." The eyes reddened again. "She just said if I didn't tell you, she'd curse me." Her voice rose as she grew frantic. "So now I've told you, and now I got to get back to work before I lose my job."

Taz got to his feet quickly and took her arm to steady her, calm her. "You'll get there," he assured her. "Just tell me where this old woman is, okay? I don't want to end up getting lost in that swamp."

She smiled up at him, and pointed. "Right the other side of that cotton. You go up the road a little, there's another road that goes right through the field. Farmer's road. Dirt and all, it's not very wide. You get to the other side, that's Swampline

Road, and you turn north, she's only a little ways up. You can't miss it; it's the only house there."

Taz thanked her, told her he'd walk her to her car, if that was all right with her boyfriend.

She giggled. "That's okay, it's out back."

Proctor stood as she turned to go. "Thank you, Erlene. I appreciate what you've done."

"Sure." A hesitation. "She knows you, Mr. Proctor," she said again. "I know she does, because she knows your name."

"But I don't know hers."

"We call her Madam," Erlene said, sidestepping toward the exit. "But her name is Riza Noscu."

He watched her hasten away and couldn't help a grin because she reminded him of one of the chipmunks he had complained about the other day. And he knew why she had parked in back—because she didn't want Bobby Grace to see her.

Which meant she hadn't told him about this message.

Taz clapped his hands quietly and rubbed his palms together. "So we get lunch and go, right? Or should we wait?"

"Sit down," Proctor answered. "Both of you. I have to tell you about a dream."

Vivian sat alone in her room.

After Erlene had left, she had simply walked

away, taken the stairs up, locked the door behind and closed the connecting door to Proctor's room.

She would not look out, would not look to the place where Taz claimed there was a swamp. She stared at the blank television screen and tried to understand what had happened downstairs. She had listened to the girl's message, had seen Proctor's barely concealed startled reaction; she had listened to the story of his dream; she had watched Taz grow upset and asked to be excused.

For a moment, as she sat there, she considered calling Taylor. She did not because she hadn't the slightest idea what to say.

A year ago she would have told both men that they were clearly out of their minds, seriously considering visiting an old woman . . . an old witch woman, for crying out loud . . . to have a serious conversation about a werewolf. For crying out loud.

But a lot had happened in the past year. Somehow she had been kidnapped to another world, and she didn't like it. It looked like the old world; it had the same people as the old world; it smelled and tasted and sounded like the old world.

But now there were additions.

She had seen them herself. Once.

And once had been enough.

But not in Proctor's world. Once became twice

became God knew how many times, and he never blinked.

In the old world she was under orders to protect him; in this new world the orders stood, but she had never trained for those "additions," never figured she had to be able to use her skills against them.

I need time, she thought; I need more time to understand.

She bowed her head, stared at the carpet.

The hell of it was, there was no more time. The old world was gone forever, and damn Proctor, she was afraid.

There were still blue gaps in the clouds, but Taz had to look hard to find them. When he did, they were so small he almost wished they weren't there. It would be easier just to have all the clouds. It fit better. Much better.

Hands deep in his pockets he walked around the empty back parking lot. There wasn't a whole lot to think about, but he wanted time to do it anyway, and Proctor had given it to him. As much, the man said, as he needed.

The dream hadn't surprised him.

He had met Petra in Atlantic City, and by the time that episode had ended, there wasn't anything about her that would surprise him.

What bothered him was the warning. As it should, and he knew it. Still, as he stared blindly across the empty field behind the motel, he could not help an unreasonable surge of anger at the unfairness of it all. He had been joking with Vivian about the greedy landlord . . . but not entirely.

His own cases were one thing, and that was okay. That's what he was good at.

But every time he worked with Proctor . . .

He kicked at a stone, missed it, and swore.

This was no investigation. Proctor hadn't even made a pretense of seriously considering this . . . this thing was actually a serial killer. He had accepted the existence of the creature as soon as they landed in Alton, maybe even before. All that talk about possible this and possible that, all that bull about this peripheral stuff . . . talk, nothing but talk.

This was no investigation.

This was a hunt.

*listen to her or you're all going to die*

He whirled and glared at the motel. He picked up a stone, whirled again, and threw it as hard as he could into the field.

Son of a bitch, I don't want to do this.

He wiped an angry hand over his face.

I don't want to end up like Doc.

He reached for another stone, was about to throw it after the first one, when he saw a man making his way through the weeds toward him. His clothes looked like they'd been through a slice-and-dice machine, he needed a shave at least a week ago, and he was mumbling to himself.

"Great," Taz said. "Just what the hell I need right now."

He turned his back on the man, put his hands back in his pockets, and decided he might as well get back, Proctor would be wondering.

"Hey!"

He rolled his eyes and kept walking.

"Hey, you, kid!"

He couldn't help it; he looked over his shoulder.

The man waved at him, asking him to wait. Then he fell, took a few seconds to get back on his feet, and waved again.

Jesus, Taz thought; why me, huh? Why me?

Closer, and the man didn't have to yell. "Hey, kid, are you staying at this place?"

Taz didn't answer.

"Are you visiting?" He had almost reached the field's end. "You don't look like you're local."

"Yes, I am, and no, I'm not, and I'm busy," Taz said curtly.

"North." The man grinned. "You're from up North." He stumbled onto the blacktop, stood panting, still grinning. His hair was a matted grey, his dirty face lined, and he kept his left arm against his coat as though keeping something from falling out. "You are, aren't you? From up North?"

Warily Taz nodded.

"Wouldn't happen to be from New Jersey, would you?"

Taz didn't know why, but there was something about the guy that made him say, eyes wide, "Are you . . . God damn, are you Garber Kranz?"

Suddenly the man sobered. "Black Oak?"

Taz nodded, stunned.

"We have to get inside, son. I need to talk with your boss before they catch me."

# FOURTEEN

Proctor had pushed the table against the wall, and sat in the desk chair with his back to the windows. Vivian was on his left in an armchair, glancing at the window, at him, back to the window. The light continued to fade as the clouds continued to join, but he did not turn on the lamps. The brightest object in the room was the window.

"You do that deliberately," she had said while he rearranged the furniture. Taz would be on his right, forcing the old man to sit on the edge of the bed, directly in front of Proctor, facing into the light.

"Sometimes," he had answered. "Sometimes."

"What about the thunder?"

He smiled; she didn't smile back.

The old man was in the bathroom, cleaning up as best he could, apologizing the whole time for his appearance. Taz leaned against the bathroom door's frame, maintaining the initial contact, his tone suggesting there was no hurry, take your time, you're among friends.

There had been nothing concealed under the shabby raincoat; the old man was sure he had broken a rib in a fall the night before.

While Kranz was at the sink, Taz leaning against the doorframe, Proctor turned to Vivian and said, "I don't want to have to worry about you."

Her eyes widened slightly. "You don't have to."

"Yes, I do." He tilted his head toward Taz. "Him, too. He's pissed off because this is another bad one."

"You mean real?"

"Yes."

"How do you know? How can you know?"

"My mother used to say, 'Ask a stupid question . . .'"

"I don't think it's a stupid question."

Proctor stared at her until she looked away, but not before he saw the grin. "If I could tell you things, I would. It would make life a lot easier, at least around me. But I can't."

"So I've noticed," she said dryly.

She was too far away to touch. "Vivian."

She looked back.

"What you and I have seen . . . what you did . . . you want that to be an exception to what you know. And you know that it isn't. Not anymore. If I could help you with that, I would. I can't. This is the way it is."

She slumped back in her chair, puffed her cheeks and blew a long slow breath. "You read minds, too, don't you."

"No, I don't think so."

"Then how did you know? About what I was thinking?" She shook her head; no need to answer. All she said was, "It's hard."

All he answered was, "I know."

A brief spell of coughing and a groan interrupted them. Proctor winced in empathy for Kranz's injury, watched Taz reach into the bathroom, a helping hand.

Proctor chuckled softly.

"What?" Vivian demanded.

"It's perverse."

"No surprise. So . . . what?"

"If it's not a shapeshifter," he said, "I'll be so glad I'm wrong you have no idea."

"No more than me, Proctor."

"But if it is a werewolf, there are two things." He held up a finger. "First, Eriko will be thrilled, because we've hit the first of the Great Monster Triangle." He held up a second. "And if it's a werewolf, we don't have to learn how to fight it. We already know."

Vivian stared at him as if he were crazy.

He shook his head, watching Taz step back to

make way for the retired teacher. "Jeez, Viv, don't you ever watch the movies?"

"Vivian, never Viv," she reminded him, mocking and exaggerating the tone he used when he corrected others with his name.

Their laughter, though restrained, made Taz frown as he sat, motioning Kranz to the bed. "What the hell is so funny?"

"Life, Taz," said Proctor. "Just life." Then, to the old man: "Mr. Kranz, you know why I'm here, and it looks like you were right—Maudie Batts and Maude Tackett could well be the same woman. I thank you for the information, even if it is a bit late. But that doesn't explain why you're hiding." He opened a hand—*your turn*.

Kranz sat as straight as he could, trying to keep pressure off his ribs. His white hair had been slicked back, his face and hands washed. He hadn't shaved, and there was little to be done about his clothes; they looked as though he had had to sleep in them. One sleeve was torn from elbow to cuff, one knee of his trousers had been scraped away, and his old shoes could have been run over several times by a truck. The shirt's top button was fastened, but there was no tie.

There was silence in the room.

"Mr. Kranz?"

The old man's lips worked as if he were toothless—pursed, then sucked in, pursed again. In and out. A low smacking sound. In and out.

Proctor didn't move. He kept his hands on the armrests, his legs crossed at the knee. When Taz shifted, he lifted a finger to keep him quiet.

"Mr. Kranz."

Kranz jumped, shook his head hard, rubbed a hand over his face. An embarrassed smile for the room, and for a space over Proctor's right shoulder. He stared at it for several long seconds, lowered his gaze and cleared his throat three times. Grimaced and rubbed his side lightly.

Pursed his lips.

In and out.

Proctor leaned forward. Gently: "Mr. Kranz."

The voice was tenor high and smooth: "They're after me."

"Yes."

A tremulous smile: "I've gotten away, but they're after me."

"I know."

Kranz pressed a finger to his eye, held it there, rubbed the eye, dropped the hand into his lap. "I think . . . I think it's Royal's fault."

Taz shook his head in bewilderment. He didn't understand what had happened. A signal from Proctor told him to be patient.

"We saw your home, Mr. Kranz. I'm very sorry."

"I heard it on the radio," Kranz said. "Royal was my best friend." He swiped a quivering finger under one eye; there was no tear. His gaze drifted back to the window over Proctor's left shoulder. "They were after me before that, of course, but I didn't think . . . I never thought . . ."

Vivian stirred now; a signal to her, too.

The muted prolonged rumble of a series of trucks heading west along the highway; the rustle of the coverlet as the old man shifted uneasily.

Then:

I'm a teacher. That's all I do. I'm just a teacher. I'm retired, but I still teach a little. Kids who want to know more. I teach science. Royal wanted to be an archeologist, so I found him books and magazines and ways to get on digs. He's a natural prowler. He likes to . . . dear Lord . . . Maudie opened that silly little store about four, five years ago. I don't know how she lived because hardly anyone ever went there. Kids liked her, the adults didn't. She claimed to be a New Age witch, all the crystal and tarot paraphernalia.

I don't know how she lived.

Then Royal . . . a month ago, perhaps. A month, I think. I could look it up. I'm retired, you know, but I like to keep a schedule. Most of the time. It helps me to remember. So I keep the schedule. Royal teases me about . . . dear Lord.

A month ago, it was near the beginning of March, he had an idea that he might find remains of an encampment in the Lakochebala. That's all he would tell me. He liked to surprise me, you see. He wouldn't tell me any more in case he was wrong. But he told me that much, and so I encouraged him, as I always do. For a man with little schooling, he . . . was a remarkably intelligent man.

I do not, Mr. Proctor, blame him in any way. You must understand that. I do not blame him for what has happened.

I don't remember how long he was gone. I could look it up, I suppose. I kept records for him. He forgets, sometimes, that you need records so you won't be cheated if you find something important. He didn't care, not Royal. But I did. I certainly did. Give him his due is my motto. Give him his due.

And that old devil, that old dog, wouldn't you know but that he got up and found something. He kept it for a while, said he was going to study it. Said he wanted to . . . study it.

Lips pursed; sucked in.

Taz looked to the window. Nothing there but the dim light the clouds permitted the afternoon, save where falls of sunlight still landed from the shrinking blue.

Proctor didn't move.

Kranz ran a finger from one eye, down his cheek to his jaw, pulled the finger away and examined it. Repeated the action with the other eye and cheek, examined the finger again, squinting so hard his eyes nearly vanished in the folds of his face. He didn't find what he sought, so he placed the hand on his knee.

"Mr. Kranz."

The old man nodded; he was listening.

"Mr. Kranz, what did Royal find?"

"They're after me."

"Yes."

Kranz wiped the back of a hand over his mouth and swallowed; it was difficult, but he swallowed. Vivian rose easily to her feet and fetched a glass of water from the bathroom. The man accepted it with a vacant smile and drank until the glass was empty. Coughed. And grimaced.

Sighed and:

I do not know what it is that Royal found. I have seen it. I have it. But I do not know what it is.

We were puzzled, Royal and I, but he had already found what he called clues—he always called them clues, not signs or indications; he always called them clues—to a new pursuit. Something entirely different. He stayed in town for a week or so, reading I don't know what, and then packed up his car and left.

I never saw him again.

But not long after he presented me with this most puzzling surprise, that's when it began.

Dear Lord, those poor animals. Those poor, poor children.

They came to my house at night and tried to break in, but I am, for a teacher of my years, rather handy with weapons, and I drove them away. I do not know who they were, but I am not such a fool that I did not, eventually, realize what they were after.

I am a decent shot, Mr. Proctor, but I am also older than I used to be, and in a fight face-to-face there was no question I would lose. So I ran away.

I shall be judged a coward, but I ran away.

Kranz bent over, hands clasped between his legs, his hair as it dried spreading, and falling in wisps over his ears and his face. When he looked up, it was not at the space over Proctor's shoulder, but at Proctor.

"God help us, I saw what happened to Johnny Verlin."

His voice had changed from tenor to nearly shrill, and the man who sat there now was a score of years older than the man who hailed Taz from the field. His lips trembled, his eyes filled with tears, a bubble of spittle quivered at the corner of his mouth.

He licked his lips.

"They are after me, you know."

Proctor watched him, did not move.

"I have looked upon their god, and they are after me."

Proctor shook his head. "Not because of what you saw, sir."

Kranz appeared to consider this, cocking his head side to side like an aged bird. "Perhaps you're right." He smiled. "Perhaps you are right."

Proctor closed his eyes briefly, inhaled and held it, released it in a sigh.

The old man's smile was touched with madness.

"Mr. Kranz."

Kranz sat up, carefully, wincing. "Damn, but it hurts."

"It will for a while."

"Yes. I've done this before, young man. I'll be hurting for days."

"You want me to look at it?" Taz asked. "You know, maybe I can—"

"No," the old man snapped. "I am perfectly capable of looking after myself."

Proctor nodded. "Mr. Kranz, whoever wants to hurt you searched your house."

"I know. I snuck back there last night. What a terrible mess. It will take me weeks to get it back to normal. I'm going to have to tell the school I can't work for a while." He touched his side gingerly. "This, and the cleaning . . . weeks, it will take weeks."

"Do you still have what Royal gave you?"

Kranz laughed, a hollow sound deep in his chest. "Yes. And no." Suddenly he winked at Vivian. "I have it, but not in my possession."

"Hidden," Proctor said, regaining his attention.

"Of course."

"Where?"

The old man leaned away, shaking his head. "I'm not going. I will not go. Absolutely not. They are—"

"You won't have to," Proctor promised, a hand up to calm him. "We will. But we have to know what it is, so we'll know it when we see it. And where it is, how to get there."

"Yes." Kranz bobbed his head. "Yes, very wise. They won't be expecting you. They are after me." His eyes widened. "But my house—"

Vivian smiled and said, "You'll be right here, Mr. Kranz. No one will know. You can sleep."

"Thank you, my dear, but I do not think I will ever sleep again." An awkward bow. "But I will, however, accept your kind invitation." He looked around the room, approving. "I will be all right here."

"Yes, you will, sir."

"They're after me, you know. I have seen their god, and they are after me."

Vivian's smile held, but barely.

"Mr. Kranz," Proctor said, standing slowly,

"Taz here is going to get you something to eat. While he's gone, I'll need you to do me a favor."

"I will help wherever I can, sir."

"Good. I need you to tell me what you found, what it is that you think these people want, and I need directions on how to get to it."

Kranz almost rose himself, changed his mind, and held out a hand instead, wiggling his fingers until Vivian handed him a notepad from the desk.

"Do you know how to row a boat, Mr. Proctor?" he asked.

"Yes, sir, I do."

"Good, because you'll need to when you go into the Lakochebala."

# FIFTEEN

Erlene Hotchkiss wandered up and down the empty terminal, humming, whirling slowly as if she were waltzing, all the while keeping one hand on the leather pouch that hung beneath her uniform. Her shoes squeaked on the floor. The recessed lights cast a half dozen shadows of herself, shadows that danced with her.

"Erlene," Dee called from her station, "will you stop that? It's not right. It's not respectful."

Erlene grinned. She didn't care if it was right, and she would get over it not being respectful. She had indeed gone to Dee's house after leaving Madam the old Witch, and she indeed had gotten her self good and properly drunk. And being good and properly drunk she had been stupid enough to drive home. In the middle of the night.

And when she heard just a few minutes ago from a departing passenger that they had found Cooper Brock's body in the pines that morning, the first thing she had done was shed a tear. Then she figured she must have been on the road about the same time. Which meant, make all the fun you want, that the charm worked.

"Erlene, for God's sake!"

"I am," Erlene declared, "dancing in his honor. He would have liked that, don't you think?"

"You hardly knew him."

Erlene laughed. "Doesn't matter, honey. I'm still doing it for him."

Of course she was making herself dizzy, and was glad when Bobby came through the front doors. It gave her an excuse to wobble over to him and throw her arms around him. "Been dancing," she announced. "I'm dizzy." And she giggled.

Bobby grabbed her arms and pushed her away. "Christ, Erlene, you drunk or something?"

Hurt but not crushed, she noticed the look on his face, the funny way he held himself. "Bobby, something wrong?"

He shrugged. "Nah, not really. One of those wiseass protesters caught me a good one in the ribs with his sign, that's all."

"Oh, Bobby!"

"No big deal. I caught him a good one with my boot, and now he's crying his eyes out in a cell."

Erlene shook her head in mild scolding. "Reverend Carlton's gonna be on your ass for that, Bobby."

Bobby scoffed, and straightened his hat. "Like I care, you know? That old black—"

"Bobby!"

For a second, she thought he would hit her the way his face changed, red and hard. Then he ducked his head and muttered an "I'm sorry, Erlene. You know how it is."

Erlene looked over at Dee, who rolled her eyes.

"Well, maybe I'll forgive you if you take me dancing tonight."

"Can't."

"Again?"

He grinned. "You know how it is, darlin'. Big moon, all the nuts are out."

"Jesus, Bobby," Dee said disgustedly, "don't you ever think before you talk?"

Proctor stood at the door, denim jacket in his hand even though he knew it was too warm for it outside; he carried it for the holster sewed into the lining. He watched the old man seated at the desk, a lunch tray in front of him. The food hadn't been touched even though Proctor was sure Kranz had to be hungry.

"I'll be back soon," he said. "You'll be all right here."

With a fork Kranz poked at his salad.

"Mr. Kranz."

The old man turned his head slowly. "Do you have any idea what it's like to be crazy?"

* * *

Mayor Posten sat at his desk, elbows on the blotter, head resting on his palms. He didn't know what to do, didn't know what to say . . . not to the press, not to anyone. It did no good to point out that Cooper, by being where he was for whatever reason he was out there, was as good as painting a KILL ME sign on his back. The horrible fact was, the boy was dead. Just like the others. And right now, just like yesterday, that old blowhard Reverend Carlton was in the street. Only this time he had a bullhorn, and this time there was more than his congregation with him. Hundreds of them. Like magic they were there soon as word got out, which it wasn't supposed to because he'd made Arthur swear he would keep his men quiet. Hundreds of those people, praying at the tops of their voices, singing hymns, and working themselves up to storming the building and stringing him up.

He had checked the window a little bit ago, and damned if there weren't a bunch of actual, honest-to-God torches in the back of someone's truck. Those sons of bitches were planning to stay all damn night.

He moaned.

He looked at the telephone and wished he had the nerve to call the governor and admit defeat, send in the troops and the state boys, we can't handle nothing down here anymore.

The fact was, as Arthur so plainly explained not an hour ago, the state boys will probably be down here anyway, taking over whether he liked it or not. Posten could not figure out which was the better publicity, though—the call or the takeover.

He moaned louder, and didn't raise his head when the door swung open. "What?" he demanded.

"We got more trouble."

Arthur. Mr. Chief of Police Macbain. Mr. Good News himself.

He said, "Shit, what is it now?"

"Some of those folks, they got it in their head this is somehow Madam Noscu's fault."

"Oh, Christ."

"I don't know how many, but they're about ready to head out there."

Posten sat back heavily, slapped his hands on the desk. "Well, goddamnit, don't tell me about it, do something about it." His eyes closed; when they opened, the fat bastard was still there. "This is that werewolf crap, right?"

The chief nodded.

Posten scrubbed his chin with the heel of one hand. "Who would have thought, this day and age, we'd have actual people believing in actual people who walk around like a wolf." He stared at the ceiling. "Jesus!"

"Richard, it could be a nut anyway. Only this one thinks he's a wolf or some kind of critter like that. It doesn't matter in the end. Shit's heading for the fan anyway."

The mayor chuckled; he couldn't help it. "You got you some of those silver bullets, Art?"

Macbain tried and failed not to smile. "Wouldn't hurt."

Posten shook his head, suddenly struck by weariness. "So you got someone going out there?"

"Yes. Just one, though. Can't spare any more than that."

"Then what?"

"Then, no offense, Mr. Mayor, but you'd better show your face out there soon, or all hell's gonna break loose."

"What did he mean?" Taz asked from the back-seat.

"He saw what killed that boy."

"But that doesn't make him crazy."

Proctor was reluctant to say more, not when Vivian sat as rigidly as she did beside him. Listening carefully. Taz, however, would not give up. He wanted to understand why Kranz seemed so normal until he began to tell his story.

"It was like, bang, all of a sudden he cracked up."

Proctor turned left onto the highway. "A guess, all right?" he said.

Taz waited.

"He was safe."

"Yeah, he was. So . . ."

A deep breath. "So he finally had a chance to think about what happened. About what he saw."

"But he thought about that before."

"He wasn't safe before, Taz."

They had gone less than a mile before Vivian said, "Yes."

From Polly Dove's front porch, Deke watched what he figured was the last of the blue get swallowed by the grey. The wind hadn't picked up, he couldn't feel that it would rain soon, but he shivered anyway, in anticipation.

He was purely lucky to be alive. He believed that. His hand lay gently on his head so he could feel the lump without really touching it. No blood; just a lump.

Purely lucky to be alive.

When he'd awakened, lying in the mud by his truck, he had been so terrified that he'd leapt in and was gone even before he had shut the door. For some reason, home seemed like the last place he wanted to be, and he ended up pounding on Polly's door. She wouldn't let him in once she smelled the beer and saw him hanging on to the frame so he couldn't fall over. With a terse, "stay there," she left him alone in the dark, returned with an old sleeping bag she tossed at him.

"On the porch," she ordered.

Meekly he had nodded, in no shape to argue.

"You didn't get him."

"No. I—"

She'd slammed the door, and he'd crawled into the bag as close to the wall as he could get. The rain hadn't reached him, but the wind had, and he thought for sure he would freeze to death before morning. When he woke shortly after dawn, amazed that he'd been able to sleep at all, he kept the sleeping bag wrapped around him like a blanket and sat on the hanging bench at the porch's end, feet on the floor to keep from swinging. Not long afterward, she had brought him a slice of buttered toast and a big mug of coffee.

Not a word.

Not a blessed word.

He ate, drank, finally sloughed off the sleeping bag, and wrinkled his nose at the stink of him. Still he didn't leave. He needed to talk to someone, and Polly was his best bet. Except she wasn't talking to him. He tried several times, knocking on the door, calling her name as friendly as he could be, but she didn't answer.

Finally, just an hour ago, he'd yelled, "Damnit, Polly, I don't want to use your yard for a john, but I will if I have to. Damnit."

When she opened the door, she said, "Come on, use my bathroom, then please leave. I have nothing to say to you."

He had, and he left, but he remained on the porch, pacing now and muttering, trying to understand what the hell was the matter with him that he just didn't up and go on home. Polly was obviously off her rocker, and he'd seen that damn gun on the kitchen table. Leaving would be the smart move, but he stayed anyway.

Maybe, he thought, because his neighborhood might be like this one—so damn quiet you'd think everyone had moved away during the night. Curtains were drawn, garage doors down, not even a dog nosing around a tree.

It spooked him.

Which made his delight all the more profound when Connie drove up, bumping up over the curb in her haste to park.

He waved, called to her, and frowned when she raced up the walk and collapsed into his arms.

"What?" he said. "What?"

"Cooper Brock," she told him, sobbing into his chest. "I can't stand it, Deke. I took one look and

I left. I can't stand it, I want to get out of this place."

He tried to offer her some comfort, but he had precious little to give. He had heard that howling, knew it wasn't part of the whack he'd gotten. He had heard it.

Then Connie leaned her head back, tears still coming, her eyes puffed and pink. "No man did that, Deke," she said, her head shaking as if she had some kind of disease. "We were wrong. No man did that."

He could not argue. "So what do we do? Leave?"

A door slammed behind him. He turned, still holding Connie, and saw Polly. "Sweet Jesus."

She wore hiking boots, baggy jeans, a baggy shirt, a cap pushed down on her head. Around her neck hung a large gold cross, and in her hand was the gun, which she pointed at his gut.

"No," she said. "We're getting in your truck and we're getting the heart of that thing that killed my Royal."

Proctor took the shortcut through the cotton field. The road, barely wider than the car, was slick with mud and filled with enough holes to make the ride feel as if he were driving across a washboard. A look into the rearview mirror. "Taz, did you think to—"

"Here," Taz answered evenly. His shirt hadn't

been tucked into his jeans, and he lifted one side to expose the holster clipped to his belt. He looked out the side window. "Fat lot of good it'll do with no silver bullets."

"We'll be back before dark."

Taz shook his head in disbelief, and resignation.

A left onto Swampline Road, bordered by huge oaks draped with Spanish moss. Farmland on the left, short weeds and tall wildflowers on the right. Vivian held the instructions Kranz had given them, checked them and told him there should be an unmarked road about half a mile up.

They passed a small house protected by pecan trees, its drab exterior made worse by the gardens that flowered along its sides.

Taz rapped on his window. "That's the what's-her-name's place, I guess. Are we going to stop?"

"Later. After we've done this."

Though he had been expecting some kind of confrontation since leaving the motel, it still took him by surprise when Taz finally exploded:

"Jesus Christ, Proctor, what the hell are you doing, huh?" Taz punched the back of Proctor's seat. "We came down to find out about Tackett, and we did. Then you want to find that guy, and that's okay, I guess, because he's the one who brought us here and he's in trouble. But what the hell are we doing, going into a goddamn swamp for something we have no idea what it is? Or if it even exists because the guy that brought us down here is cracked. Are you trying to get us killed?"

Vivian pointed with the sheet of paper, and Proctor slowed, and turned into a ragged break in the weeds. He stopped. Straight ahead the weeds and brush, high trees and low branches formed a tunnel in which little light existed. The trail was used frequently enough that the tires' passage had worn the grass to bare earth and kept the rest from growing very tall.

"Walk or ride," he said.

Taz slapped the back of his seat. "Are you listening to me?" He turned to Vivian. "Is he listening to me?"

"Ride," she said. "It's supposed to be a half a mile or so. I'd rather be in here than out there, and it doesn't look too bad anyway."

"I'm invisible," Taz said to the roof.

Proctor looked over his shoulder. "Taz, calm down. I need you." A moment. "He's a broken old man, he's frightened, and he needs us. I can't walk away."

Taz stared at him for a long time, breathing heavily, breathing slower. Finally he nodded. It was clear he didn't like it, but he nodded.

"Thank you," Proctor said.

"Just drive," Taz told him. "Just . . . drive."

# SIXTEEN

Two hundred yards later a low deadfall blocked the trail. Proctor braked, turned off the engine, and opened his door. Too many smells at once wrinkled his nose, and the humidity instantly took over his lungs. Pushing the door against the vegetation, he slid out, decided he wasn't going to bring the jacket. It was bad enough in here; wearing denim would drop him in a few steps.

The deadfall, a small trunk overgrown with vines, was easy to step over, and a few yards later he was able to see more clearly what lay ahead.

"Wow," said Taz behind him.

Proctor agreed.

The spread of dark water was at first glance ice-smooth and motionless. A step closer, however, and he saw a whirling eddy not far from the sloping shoreline, watched a trail of leaves move along a sluggish current. The trees were too high to see their tops, branches thick and foliage wide, their roots exposed as the water cut between them, some trunks smooth, others split and twisted; none that he could see grew out of solid land. Hillocks of spiky grass and flowers formed channels and bays. The water itself was tannic, too dark to judge its depth.

The light allowed by the canopy was surprisingly bright, not at all what he expected given the approaching weather.

At the end of the trail, now little more than a spongy path, a dugout with most of its bark intact had been dragged to land, with two rough-hewn paddles inside.

Proctor signaled Taz to the front, Vivian to the middle. Neither of them objected, until they realized that launching the canoelike boat would mean stepping in the water. Taz mumbled something about leeches and snakes and things that would probably drag him under, then grabbed the near end and pushed it into the swamp. The water barely covered his ankles—it would have to go deeper, or getting in would ground it.

Proctor and Vivian followed, and after several false starts that nearly capsized the boat, they were in and kneeling on the bottom. Vivian, her instructions out again, said, "Straight ahead to some kind of big rock. Go around on the right, and there'll be a line of swamp willows. What we want is right through the middle."

"What the hell does a swamp willow look like?" Taz asked.

"Kranz said they're the only trees right in front of us if we make the right turn."

"Swell. That really helps."

Despite their inexperience and the dugout's less-than-professional construction, it did not take long to develop a comfortable rhythm. There was little resistance from the currents, which allowed them to move as swiftly over the surface as they could paddle. Immediately, their shirts became soaked with sweat, attracting insects they could barely see but which bit them just the same.

Ten minutes later Vivian, the navigator, pointed at a huge boulder that rose in two humps out of the water. It was carpeted with moss and what looked like saplings, a large fernlike shrub growing on one hump's top. Proctor steered them to the right, keeping as close to it as he could.

"There," Vivian whispered.

The swamp willows grew in a ragged line left to right, one bent nearly in half, two so close together they could have been born of the same root system. There were so many other clumps and knots of vegetation that it was difficult to see any passage at all, much less through the middle.

Proctor let the dugout drift closer, staring so hard he frowned.

"There," Vivian whispered again.

He followed the line of her finger and saw a small gap in a waterfall of fronds. Trusting her judgment, he pushed the boat forward as Taz used his paddle to shove the fronds aside. Once through, he looked back and couldn't see any sign of their passage. The swamp had closed in before he'd taken a breath.

That's when he realized how silent it was.

He supposed he had been expecting the swamp to sound like a jungle, supposed he got that idea from television and the movies.

What he heard was the splash of the paddles, not very loud. A few birds so high he could not see them or find their direction. A hum of insects when they passed a floating island and later, a large patch of water lilies. A quick splash far to his left—a great blue heron catching its meal.

The rush of a high wind that made him look up, where he saw the clouds being torn away again.

They took a break and drifted.

Vivian pointed out a piling driven into the swamp's bottom. A vine choked it, and something dark swam in sinuous arcs around it.

"Take it wide," she told them. "Cottonmouth."

After each quick stroke, Taz held his paddle up like a bat. "It can't climb in, can it?"

"You want to find out?"

Proctor watched the snake, but it made no move toward the boat. It circled the post; that's all it did.

Once past, they drifted again, giving their arms and backs a rest. Giving Proctor a chance to wonder if Taz was right, that he was being a fool for pursuing something that might not even exist. He had been entranced by the swamp until he had seen the snake, the solemn beauty of it close to overwhelming. The dangers had for a moment become background—seen but never confronted

All of this—the cypress that looked like arthritic old women, the egret he saw wading near one of those rootless islands, the flash of a fat fish under the surface—was beyond his experience. This was not, by any stretch of the imagination, connected to his world.

They moved on, Vivian directing them slowly to their left while, through the trees on the right, they could see a large plain of grasses and reeds. An osprey dived for its meal. A heron stalked through the shallows.

Taz, though he did his work, could not stop gawking, grinning to himself, practically bouncing in his seat. His objections had been drowned by the allure of the Lakochebala, and while he probably knew it, he had surrendered nonetheless.

Then Vivian said, "Proctor, over there," and over a field of blossoming lily pads he saw the island and the two-story shack. Bands of sunlight gave its uneven clapboard a sickly, striped look; the trees that lurked around and over it seemed reluctant to let their branches touch it. He searched for the dock that was supposed to be there, saw it at last under the surface. The rain, he reckoned; the water level had risen.

He checked his watch, and wasn't at all happy when he realized that it had taken them well over an hour to get out here. If his muscles were any judge, it would take them much longer to return.

They pulled alongside the porch and Taz scrambled out, held the boat until the others had followed. At their weight the porch sagged perilously, water lapping halfway to the door. With Proctor's help Taz dragged the boat up and away from the now submerged edge. A sniff, a wary look at the water, and he rubbed his palms together briskly. "In and out, right? We get it, we leave."

Proctor nodded. "It's supposed to be under a floorboard in the front room. Keep an eye out for Indians or something."

"Ha," Taz said, jumping when the porch roof creaked.

The front room was nearly empty. A single table made from a door to which four legs had been attached; a single wooden chair. The walls were bare of paint, the ceiling heavily stained. The floor was made of uneven planks of different kinds of wood, splinter feathers marking the joins and the gaps. The only light came from the door and front window.

"Who the hell would live here?" Vivian wondered, treading cautiously.

"The old man said he used it for a quiet place. He doesn't know who really owns it, but he comes out here once in a while to sit, smoke a cigar, watch the critters." Proctor crouched low and poked at a floorboard. "How are we supposed to know which one?"

She made her way around the table, with a glance through a doorway that led to a back room. A board sagged and she stepped away hastily, glared at it, and shook her head.

In five minutes they had covered it all.

"How you guys doing?" Taz said from the porch.

"Nothing yet," Vivian told him disgustedly.

A huge fly flew in the window and bumped noisily around the ceiling; a board groaned upstairs.

Using the table for support, Proctor crouched

again, grimacing at the stiffness in his legs. Kneeling all that while in the boat had done him no good at all, and he prayed he wouldn't have to do any swimming, not to mention walking, anytime soon.

"This is crazy," she complained. She stared at the paper in her hand, then jammed it angrily into a pocket. "Crazy." When Proctor looked up, she shook her head. "No way am I going upstairs. I'll probably fall through the ceiling." Another look at the flooring, keeping in place. "He said the front room. This is the front room. We're going to have to pull the boards up until we find it."

Proctor smiled. "Maybe not." He pushed at the table, its legs scraping loudly across the floor. He pointed, and she saw a half board with a dark-rimmed knothole just off-center. He leaned over and tried to see inside, but the light wasn't strong enough.

"Too dark," he said. The hole wasn't large enough for his hand, so he slipped three fingers inside and tried to pull the board free.

"Snakes," she warned.

"Spiders, alligators . . ." He pulled harder, and the board gave a little. "Give me a hand."

Giving him a look that promised payback if her fingers didn't stay on her hand, she hooked two of hers in the hole, and they pulled on a count. The board protested stubbornly, but it rose slowly, then suddenly, and Proctor tossed it aside. Leaning over this time, he spotted a shadow within the darkness.

"Bingo," he whispered.

He reached in and touched it with a forefinger. Cloth; stiff cloth. After two fumbling attempts he managed to pull it out, and set it on the table.

"Well," Vivian said. "At least he wasn't lying."

"Got it," Proctor called.

Taz came to the doorway. "That's it?"

A clumsily wrapped package whose shape was uncertain, whose size was close to a foot across. The cloth felt like leather that once had been chamois soft, now stiffened by age and the elements. Stains turned patches of it an oily black; it was held together by a rawhide cord. The knot was too large and too stiff for Proctor to undo.

"We'll have to cut it."

"Not here," Vivian said. "Let's get it back first."

He agreed, tucked it under his arm like a football. "Hardly weighs anything."

"Damn," she said. "And I was hoping it was gold."

Then Taz yelled, "Oh, shit," and Proctor hurried to the door in time to see the dugout floating away.

"Taz," he said, but said it too late.

Taz stepped into the swamp, the water rising instantly to his waist, and went after it. "God," he said, holding his arms up. "Jeez, it feels like I'm walking on a sponge."

Vivian pushed Proctor aside. "Taz, damnit, get back here."

"I almost got it." He reached, and the motion pushed the water which pushed the boat farther away. "Shit. Hang on, I'll get it."

Proctor focused on the water's surface, wishing now he hadn't left his coat behind.

"Taz!" Vivian said. Then, much softer, "Proctor."

Taz lunged for the boat, yelling with triumph when he managed to snare it with one hand.

Proctor saw the ripples, a hundred feet, maybe more, beyond where Taz was waving a hand in victory and pulling the boat behind him back toward the shack.

"Guys, I—"

Frantically, Vivian waved at him to be silent with one hand while, with the other, she reached behind her and pulled out her gun. At the sight of the weapon, Taz's eyes widened and he whirled awkwardly, scanning the water, trying to find what she had seen.

The ripples widened and the alligator broke the surface, snout and eyes, ridged back and slow-moving tail. It did not appear to be very large, but that didn't matter. It moved steadily toward the boat, nudging lily pads aside.

"Keep moving, Taz," Proctor said, keeping his voice level. "Keep moving. Leave the boat and keep moving."

But Taz could not release his grip. He tried to move as fast as the water and the bottom would permit, but the boat slowed him down.

"Taz."

Vivian slipped in front of Proctor and as close to the edge of the porch as she could, so Taz and the boat would not be between her and the alligator. Water lapped over her feet.

"In the boat," Proctor said, wondering how the hell he managed to sound so calm.

Panic turned Taz around again, and this time he saw it. "Jesus, Mary, and Joseph," he said quietly.

"In the boat, Taz." This time it was Vivian, and she had taken aim.

Taz backed toward the shack, the dugout lengthwise in front of him like a shield. He was still fifty yards away, bouncing now as he worked out the best way to get aboard in one move.

The alligator moved closer. In no hurry at all.

Proctor's right hand was in a fist so tight he could feel the skin across his knuckles ready to split. It took a conscious effort to loosen it, a conscious effort to breathe.

Taz slipped and went under.

"No," Proctor yelled, and headed for the water.

Taz surfaced, sputtering, shaking his head, and throwing himself up and over and into the boat, where he lay on the bottom, shaking uncontrollably. At the same time, Vivian fired, the gunshot enormously loud. Birds fled the trees in screaming flocks, and there was frantic splashing around the island.

The alligator swam on.

Taking its time.

She fired again, and Proctor had no idea if it would do any good, how thick the creature's hide was, where its vulnerable points were.

The alligator submerged.

Vivian scowled, a faint curse before she fired one more time at the last place she had seen it.

The boat drifted, thirty yards now, and Proctor tossed the package into the shack and tossed himself into the water, ignoring Vivian's angry shouts. It was cold below, the shock of it catching his breath, but not slowing him down. The gator knew he was there, so there was no sense trying to be subtle. He used his hands and arms to propel him toward the boat, the only thing he saw until Taz raised his head. By then Proctor was there, had the blunt bow in his hands and already beginning to backpedal.

It was like running through a nightmare—legs

and lungs and arms worked, but he felt as if he weren't moving at all.

Taz stared wordlessly at him.

He stared back and did not see him.

Then Taz said, "Boss," and something brushed against his back.

# SEVENTEEN

It was the relief in Taz's voice, not his expression, that told Proctor he had bumped up against the edge of the porch. He immediately rolled out of the water and lay on his back, watching a bee make a sputtering journey from one end of the roof to the other. His head felt packed with explosives, his face hot with fever. As he lay there waiting for his body to put itself back together, he heard Vivian assure Taz that the alligator was gone, then tell him there wasn't a chance in hell he was going to paddle again. Taz made only a token protest before he asked if they wouldn't mind getting back to the car, because there was a crazy old man back at the motel whose head he personally wanted to separate from its shoulders.

Proctor laughed. Coughed. Laughed again and sat up.

The heat passed; his breathing steadied.

Within five minutes they were on their way, Taz holding the package in his lap.

The birds had returned, scolding, chattering loudly. Taz reached for his gun when he saw a dark shape floating in the water, catching himself just in time when Vivian pointed out that logs, even in Georgia, aren't dangerous to humans.

The ache soon returned to Proctor's arms, and progress was slower than their trip out. He didn't mind. He had done what he had promised, and once they reached the motel and once they had cleaned up, he was going to take Taz's advice and offer Kranz a lift out of state. Perhaps he wouldn't make it an offer after all; perhaps he would just do it. The old man needed help, and he wouldn't get it here.

He saw the plain of reeds and grass.

They spotted another alligator, huge and dry, on a bank heaped with leaves and mud. Her nest, he thought, and thanked whatever luck remained with him that such a place hadn't been on the shack island. If it had, a few measly gunshots wouldn't have kept her away from the threat to her young.

Taz, his shoulders hunched, head bowed, said nothing.

They passed the vined piling; the cottonmouth was gone.

"Rest," Vivian said, and placed her paddle across her lap.

The drift was imperceptible; it was as if they had run aground.

Proctor rubbed his face with both hands, wiped it with his forearm sleeves. He reached out and poked Taz's back. "You alive?"

Taz nodded.

"You want to quit?"

He nodded again.

"You can't. I still need you."

He heard a muffled, "Why?"

"You know damn well why," he answered lightly. "And I need someone to save me from RJ's awful lunches."

Taz didn't react.

Vivian looked over her shoulder at him, then at Proctor, and shook her head, warning him off.

All the time you need, he said silently to the young man's back; you have all the time you need.

More birds, more splashes. The bullfrogs multiplied, and there was a catlike yowling that lasted far too long.

He leaned forward automatically when he thought he heard a siren calling, its rise and fall giving him no clue as to whether it belonged to an ambulance or a police car.

On the other hand, maybe he hadn't heard it at all.

He could barely feel the beat of his own heart.

\* \* \*

He first noticed the mist when Taz, unthinking, trailed his hand across the water and stirred a pale string of white into a knot. Before he could say anything, Taz yanked his hand back and wiped it anxiously on his shirt. Another string snaked out of a hollow in the exposed roots of a cypress.

He looked up. The clouds were long gone, and so was the faded blue of the bright-sun afternoon. He checked his watch, but it had stopped at 3:00. Somehow he had grossly underestimated the time they had been in the swamp. Although he could not see the sun, he figured it couldn't be far above the horizon.

"Vivian," he said. When she looked back, he held up his wrist, tapped the watch, pointed to the sky.

Taz shifted, raised his head. "I'm not dead, you know. The sun's going down, right?"

Proctor knifed his paddle into the water. "Right."

Taz shrugged. "Gonna be tight, right?"

"Not too."

"And I'll bet we don't have a flashlight."

Proctor said, "We won't need it," all the while cursing himself for being so unprepared. This wasn't like him. Although he could not possibly prepare for all contingencies, he always made sure he had what he thought he'd need. This, however . . . charging off into a swamp—a swamp, for God's sake—without even the basics . . . this wasn't like him at all.

"It's okay," Taz said, and hiked his shirt up, exposing the holster on one side, a small black pouch on the other. He zipped it open, shook out some water, and held up a short slender red rod. A move of his thumb, and Proctor saw a bulb glow at one end. "It ain't much, but it's better than nothing."

"You amaze me," he said with a smile.

"Yeah, well . . . I race alligators for a living."

Vivian choked abruptly into a laugh that bent her over, and Taz reached out to pat her on the back until she had calmed down. "The willows," she said, pointing.

And the mist, Proctor thought.

It rose from the surface, seemed to rise through the surface from the solid black pools he saw underneath. Thin, shifting even though there was no breeze, it coasted through the grass and reeds, blurring them and taking their color in stages. The birds' cries seemed distant; the paddles' splash seemed muffled. Yet he could still hear that constant high wind, and wondered why he couldn't feel it.

The day's heat began to slip away, and his clothes felt clammy; with each thrust of the paddle his shirt felt like it was crawling across his back, wriggling under his arms.

The mist rose.

They passed through the willows without incident, and found a reservoir of speed that numbed them to the fire that burned through their arms.

Soon now, he thought; it has to be soon.

"There," Taz said, pointing hard to the right, leaning so far over he nearly capsized them.

There was no finesse in the landing. They rammed the dugout up the slope at speed, climbed out and dragged it to one side, threw the paddles in and started for the car.

The tunnel was darker, more so because the light appeared much brighter at the other end.

The mist followed, and rose again, thinning into a gauzelike fog that left speckles of water on their faces.

"I see it," Taz said.

Proctor groaned when he had to step over the deadfall, and only stared dumbly when a striped snake slithered away from his foot and into the brush. He stumbled once and stopped to catch his breath. Swung his arms slowly. Lifted his head and twisted his neck side to side.

Vivian stood with her hands flat on the car's hood, head down, lifting one leg at a time and stretching it out. She looked like a dancer preparing to perform.

Taz, the package on one hip, looked fondly at the car, and said, "I love you."

* * *

With no room to turn around, Proctor backed the car up the trail, not caring about the branches that scraped along its sides, not caring when he veered off course once and backed into a stump. Vivian sat with her head back and her eyes closed; Taz spent the time turning the package over, shaking it, glaring at it. For a moment, as they broke out of the trees into glaring sunlight, Proctor thought Taz was going to try to bite the rawhide off.

"Patience," he said, and backed onto Swampline Road, straightened, and was about to floor the accelerator. He didn't. He stopped.

"What?" Taz demanded.

Proctor looked down the long empty road, ignoring his damp clothes and the feeling that there were dozens of tiny *things* trying to burrow beneath his skin. His vision still had not completely adjusted to the daylight outside the tunnel. Dark specks swam across his eyes, darting sideways each time he blinked.

"Boss, come on."

Proctor let the car move.

*. . . not long after he presented me with this most puzzling surprise, that's when it began . . .*

He gripped the steering wheel tightly, pushed the car a little faster.

*. . . dear Lord, those poor animals . . .*

"We have to make a stop."

"You're kidding."

Vivian opened her eyes and stared at him.

"That woman. Noscu. We have to see her before we go back."

Taz reminded him that Kranz was still in their room. Alone. God only knew what he might have done, and hindsight strongly suggested one of them should have stayed behind to watch him. "He was hurt, for crying out loud. Someone should have stayed."

"No one did."

"And that's why we can't wait, Boss. We have to take this thing back, now, and make sure the old guy is okay."

He drove faster as a feeling of dread urgency was fed by the echo of the siren he had heard while they'd been in the swamp. He doubted he would have been able to hear it had it been on the highway; had it been on this road, however . . .

Faster, until Vivian sat up, frowning.

"We're stopping," he said, and his tone left no room for debate.

*. . . those poor, poor children . . .*

He pulled over to the side of the road and was out of the car almost before it had stopped. Without a look back he hurried over to the solitary house, only vaguely aware of the flowers beginning to close for the night, acutely aware of the mingling aromas of the herbs growing in clay pots and beds.

There was no bell, so he knocked, stepped back and waited. His right hand tapped his leg impatiently. He knocked again, and waited again. His left hand went to the back of his neck and rubbed absently. He walked the length of the short porch, but white curtains had been drawn and he could not see inside.

He turned the knob and the door opened; his breath hitched for a second as he half expected to see another scene of mindless destruction. A quiet sigh of relief when he saw nothing of the kind.

"Hello?"

He could see straight through to the back door; nothing moved, there was no sound but the sound of his shoe as it trod on the threshold.

"Hello? Riza Noscu?"

Footsteps behind him and fading—Taz checking the outside and the back. He felt Vivian standing at the foot of the stairs.

One more time: "Hello?"

In the dim light he could see overstuffed chairs and couches, an ornate Victorian sideboard, framed photographs on the walls and on the top of an upright piano; fringed carpets with floral designs, tassels on lampshades, a tall floor lamp of tarnished brass. A milk-glass globe covered the living-room ceiling light; a stag's head mounted on the wall over a couch; an elephant-foot umbrella stand with two canes, no umbrellas.

*listen to her, Proctor*

Scented candles and herbs, spices and . . .

He closed his eyes. "Damnit," he said.

Quickly Vivian came up behind him.

He ignored the front room, walked down the short hall into the kitchen, where he found her on the floor in front of an old refrigerator, a chair tipped over beside her. She lay on her side, her mouth and eyes open, and when he shoved the chair aside and knelt beside her, he could hear a fading rasping.

Blood stained the front of her dress.

"My God," Vivian said. "Was it—"

"No," Proctor told her. "She's been shot."

"I'll get a doctor."

"Too late."

"But she's still alive."

"Not for long."

Madam Noscu moaned, blinked heavily, and her good eye tried to focus on him. Her head trembled and she tried to push him away. He grabbed her hand and held it, bent over and whispered, "It's all right. I come from Petra."

Her hand gripped his then and squeezed; her lips moved, but she could not speak.

Frustrated, angry that he had not listened to the others and stopped here first, he rocked back on his heels, rocked forward, and whispered, "Can you help me?"

She pulled his hand to her chest and pressed it there, watched him until he felt the lump beneath her clothes. Then a long, very long sigh, and her eyes closed, her fingers relaxed.

"Proctor," Vivian said.

There were no buttons on the front of her dress, the neckline snug against her throat.

"Get me a sharp knife."

"Proctor."

"Now, Vivian, please. Hurry."

A drawer opened to the rattle of silverware; a steak knife appeared over his shoulder, and he grabbed it, used it to cut through the material just enough for him to pull out a dark green velvet pouch on a green-velvet cord. He cut the cord and sat back, closed his eyes and said, "I'm sorry," before he stood.

"What is it?"

"I don't know." He handed her the knife, which she wiped off with a towel hanging from one of the cabinet handles. "We'll find out later."

They hurried back to the car, where Taz waited, checking the road in both directions, anxious to be on his way.

"Well?" he asked once they were inside and moving.

"She was murdered," Vivian said tightly. "Shot."

"Jesus, we got a shooter now too?"

And Proctor said, "No, I don't think so."

# EIGHTEEN

Vivian braced herself against the dashboard as Proctor swung sharply into the cotton field shortcut, fishtailing before the tires found their purchase, and shot the vehicle toward the highway. What he wanted was some time. That's all. Ten minutes alone to think without interruption. Ten minutes. Ten lousy minutes.

The sun had already dropped below the roof of the Southview Inn, and the evening's first shadows had already begun to make their way toward him, spreading like the swamp mist. A few early stars. The ghost of the moon.

When he barreled onto Alton Road he cut off a panel truck whose angry horn followed him all the way to the motel driveway, which he took just as hard, tapping the brakes so he wouldn't skid, aiming for the parking slot nearest the entrance. He had just reached the end when Taz yelled, and a run-down pickup ran at him from the left. He swung the wheel hard, but the truck caught him at the back, ripping off the rear bumper, spinning him completely around.

When he stopped the motel was at his back, and Taz was already out, screaming obscenities, flapping his arms and kicking at the blacktop.

"You okay?" he asked Vivian.

She nodded. "Yes, I think so."

The pickup had stopped on the other side of the small lot, steam billowing from beneath the hood. Taz stomped toward it, and the driver's door opened to let a huge man out.

"Oh, boy," Proctor said. He jerked a thumb toward the backseat. "Take that upstairs, okay? And see about Kranz. I'll do what I can to stop Taz from getting killed."

He didn't wait for an answer. He pushed open his door and got to his feet, grabbed the roof for a second when the world tilted side to side before righting itself. By the time he felt he could walk without falling over, Taz was at the other driver's side, demanding to know what the hell he thought he was doing, driving that way in a parking lot, didn't he know he could kill someone that way?

Proctor admired the way the man ignored him. He reached into the truck's bed, pulled out a rag, and, gently shouldering Taz aside, used it to lift the hood. Instantly he was enveloped in an explosion of steam that dissipated almost as fast as it appeared.

"Now, damnit, Polly," he said to someone in the cab, "I told you this old heap couldn't take much more." He kicked the front tire. "Damnit, I told you."

Taz reached out for the man's arm, but Proctor got there first, taking the younger man's wrist and pulling him away. "Calm down," he ordered, and said it again when Taz opened his mouth to point out the obvious—that the blacktop glittered with broken glass and pieces of the bumper. The desk clerk had come to the door, and Proctor nodded at him. "Don't let anyone out here, if you can. Tell them no one's hurt, we're just working out the insurance."

Sullen, face flushed, Taz stepped aside, balking, but finally turned and left to do as he'd been bidden.

Surprisingly the man didn't appear to be angry, at least not at him. When Proctor approached, he spread his hands helplessly. "Mister, I'm real sorry about that. I know you ain't gonna believe it when I tell you it ain't my fault. Well, it is, but it isn't."

Proctor saw two women in the cab, one in a nurse's uniform, the other wearing a baseball cap.

"That's okay," Proctor said. "I think we were both—"

"Goddamnit, Deke, get in here now!"

Deke sighed. "Mister, look, I'm really sorry, but if I don't—"

"Deke," the woman warned, and Proctor saw the gun. He also saw that, as angry as the woman sounded, it wasn't mirrored in her face.

"Problem?" he asked quietly.

"Mister, you don't know the half of it." Then he leaned away, as if seeing him for the first time. "Hey, you from up North?"

"As a matter of fact."

"You that guy looking for Maudie?"

Proctor stared at him. "How did you know that?"

Deke grinned. "Mister, this ain't exactly a small town anymore, but it's still a small town, if you know what I mean." He lowered his voice. "Don't worry about Polly. She's got herself in a knot, see, because . . . well, because her boyfriend was the guy who was killed the other night. You hear about that?"

Proctor looked at him, looked over at Polly Dove. "You mean Blondell?"

Suddenly she was at the door, one leg out, her free hand on the top of the steering wheel. "You know my Royal?" she demanded, the gun in her lap. "You know my Royal?"

Proctor hooked his thumbs into his pockets and walked toward her slowly, not letting the gun out of his sight. "I didn't know him personally, no."

She frowned, unsure. "Then how do you know him?"

"Heard a lot about him," he answered, stopping a few feet from the truck. His voice was quiet, steady. "I guess you're after his killer."

"I want its heart."

"Yeah. Yeah, I guess you would." He hadn't missed what she'd said, and he debated for a few seconds before he leaned closer, with a smile, and said, "But unless you've got silver bullets in that thing, I don't think it's going to do you any good."

The nurse gaped at him.

He heard Deke suck in a sharp breath.

Polly turned until both legs hung out of the cab, her head down. "No," she said at last. "I don't suppose it will."

He heard the tears before he saw them.

A blink, and Deke had taken the gun, and the nurse had cupped her hands over Polly's shoulders for whatever comfort the gesture offered.

Deke slumped against the truck. "Thanks, mister."

"Proctor is fine."

"Okay. Sure." A shrug. "But look, do you . . . I mean, I don't want to offend you or anything, but that stuff . . . you know." He looked at Polly and shook his head.

"Deke," the nurse snapped, "you know damn well you believe it too. You're just too scared to say it out loud." Still holding Polly's shoulders, she looked at Proctor. "The thing is, Mr. Proctor, I know it's true. I've seen the bodies. I've seen the reports."

A dozen questions tongue-tied Proctor until, finally, he decided he needed to talk to these people some more.

"Tell you what," he said, and waved at the debris. "What do you say we clean this mess up, and I'll treat you to dinner." He grinned. "This place isn't fancy, but the food's not half-bad."

Polly felt too ashamed, insisted they leave her in the truck until it was time to leave, but Proctor wouldn't relent. He wanted her to understand that every bit of information he had would take him one step closer to stopping this creature. In the end it was Connie, the nurse, who convinced her, and walked with her into the motel, Deke trailing so he could get some brooms and a trash bin from the management.

Proctor remained in the parking lot, increasingly aware of how bizarre the situation was. A town not backward by any means beset by a series of vicious killings which not a few people honestly believed were caused by a supernatural agent. And he stood in the parking lot of a motel and had a serious conversation about it with three very ordinary people.

As if, he thought, they were talking about what a mess the traffic was.

It was, he decided, more than a little surreal.

As he returned to the car to get his jacket, Vivian hurried out of the building.

He did not need to ask; if pressed he would have said he had already known.

"You looked everywhere, right?" he said before she could speak.

She didn't miss a beat. "Yes. I wanted to make sure before I told you."

"He take anything from the room?"

"No. Nothing's gone. Not even that lunch. I don't think he ate a thing." After he told her what Deke and the women had said, and what he wanted to do, she wondered what, exactly, he could get from them that would be useful.

"I don't know, but I'll know it when I hear it."

"What about the police?"

"Because of this?"

She shook her head.

"I'm not calling about Madam Noscu, if that's what you mean. They'll have too many questions, and I'm too tired and sore to think up decent answers."

"Lies, you mean," she said with a sardonic smile.

"Whatever. Besides, it will take too long." A pointed look at the darkening sky was explanation enough.

"But Proctor, she's—"

"Dead," he said flatly. "And I want to see if we can stop others from ending up that way, too."

Dinner wasn't much help.

Taz was the only one who ordered a full meal. The others had sandwiches or salads, and no one, save Taz, ate very much; they were far too preoccupied by the failing light outside. Finally, Polly began to weep, and asked for someone to please take her home. With apologies, Deke gathered her up and took her into the lobby, where he called a friend for a ride. Connie excused herself to the ladies' room, and when she returned, Proctor walked with her to the exit.

"I'm sorry I wasn't more help," she said.

"That's all right. I know more than I did before, and that's all I can really ask."

She gave him an odd look then. "Do you . . . this is going to sound dumb, but do you do this sort of thing for a living? Hunt monsters, I mean."

He laughed, and said, "No. Not really. In my job, the monsters I usually see are very human."

They stood at the glass door, watching Deke and Polly remove some things from the pickup's bed. A car turned into the driveway, its headlamps already on, and the driver hit his horn briefly, twice.

Connie shook Proctor's hand, then, and bade him a good night. "I wanted to help more, so I'm sorry again. But at least poor Cooper got in his licks." She gave him a shy smile and left, calling out to Polly as she hurried across the parking lot.

Damn, Proctor thought and turned away, looking for Vivian or Taz so they could get upstairs and—

He froze.

"Did what?" he whispered, spun, and raced out of the building, yelling, waving his arms, and slowing almost immediately when he realized Connie hadn't yet gotten into the car. She looked at him apprehensively, grasping the back door's handle, pulling the door slightly open.

Proctor pointed. "What did you just say to me?"

"I'm sorry?"

"About the Brock boy. You said he got in his licks?"

"Oh, that." She lowered her voice as if what she was about to say was a secret not to be divulged. "When they found him, he had this big silver cross in one hand. About four or five inches, kind of pointy at the bottom. Dr. Oraden, I told you about him, he wondered about the blood that was all over it, see, so he tested. It was not the same as Cooper's. So he must've fought back, you know?" She made a stabbing motion with her hand, and nodded sharply. "So if we're all wrong about this stuff, we've got the DNA to convict the real killer."

Proctor thanked her again, and walked slowly back. Sometimes all the planning in the world isn't equal to one stroke of decent luck.

Vivian and Taz waited at the door, and when they saw his face, Taz said uncertainly, "What's up?"

Proctor's smile was not pleasant.

"He's wounded. The son of a bitch is wounded."

"But that doesn't help," Vivian said. "We can't go checking on everyone in town."

"We don't have to," he told her. "He's already come to us." He started for the stairs. "We already know who he is."

# NINETEEN

The lamps were on, and Proctor sat at the desk. In front of him the velvet pouch lay open, spread and flattened. Against the dark green background, the silver bullets were so smooth, so new, they seemed artificial. He hadn't really been surprised when he opened the pouch and saw its contents; he had felt them when he'd first taken the pouch from Madam Noscu's neck. But he knew there should have been so much more—a tale, a reason, a story of some legend, a story of magic.

His fault.

She was dead because of him, and all he had left were these six silver bullets.

"Two for each of us," he said. "Two each."

Vivian stood at the window; Taz sprawled in an armchair. They didn't move.

Proctor pushed away from the desk and walked over to his bed. With a knife he had swiped from the restaurant he poked at the package they had retrieved from the Lakochebala. Then, with a look to the others, he sawed through the rawhide cord and peeled and cut away the stiff cloth.

The only sound in the room was his harsh breathing.

When the last of the cloth fell away, the package much smaller now, he dropped the knife and sat hard on the bed behind him.

"Proctor," Vivian said.

"I know. I know."

Smaller than a softball, larger than a baseball, it was an uneven globe of amber crystal. If there was something embedded inside, he could not see it, but it took in the room's light and created shadows beneath the surface.

"Kansas," she whispered.

He agreed. "Kansas."

He knelt on the floor and inched closer, peering into it, reaching out a finger and pulling it back, wiping it on his jeans, curling it toward his palm. The globe made no sound, was not a light source of its own. Nevertheless, the old man had said that the killings hadn't begun until Royal Blondell had brought it home.

Coincidence, he thought, has no meaning here.

Suddenly he was on his feet. "Pack," he said as he rewrapped the globe, making sure he did not touch any part of its surface. "Everything. Pack. I'll put this in my suitcase. Vivian, call Atlanta and get that plane back down here. As soon as we're done, we're out of here, understand?"

In ten minutes they were ready; five minutes after that, he had explained again everything the nurse had told him, repeating her pantomime of the way Cooper Brock had tried to defend himself.

"In the side or shoulder," he said. "That's where it was wounded. The side or shoulder."

"Jesus, the old man," Taz said. "He wouldn't let me help him with his ribs."

"Or," said Vivian, "that officious prick of a cop."

Proctor nodded, pleased that someone else had noticed how stiff and a little awkward Grace had been. That second day, he had also wondered why the cop hadn't taken the stairs after delivering his invitation from the chief. A young man like that, strutting and preening, does not take an elevator to go one floor down.

"But which?" Taz wanted to know. "I mean, the old man was really upset about it. The dying, I mean. I don't think he was faking it." He scratched through his hair. "Can you be one of these things and not know it?"

Proctor went to the window.

Darker now, and the moon brighter, almost full.

He smiled mirthlessly, remembering some lines from one of his favorite old movies:

*Even a man who is pure at heart*
*And says his prayers at night . . .*

"No. This is not a matter of splitting yourself off into another physical being, so that one exists independent of the other." He turned his back on the night. "There is a transformation, but not a separation. You don't go to bed one night, have bad dreams, and wake up the next day without knowing what you've done."

"You know what you are, Taz. You know."

"What about you, Proctor?" Vivian asked softly. "Do you know who it is?"

"Yeah," he said, nodding slowly. "Yeah, I think I do."

Deke sat in the dark living room, his arms around Polly, who had finally cried herself to sleep. Connie's apartment was pretty nice, but he didn't think he could stand listening to neighbors tromp overhead all the time. Not now, anyway. Especially not now.

Connie walked into the room for about the fifth time in ten minutes, dropped a fork onto the coffee table, and looked around with her hands on her hips. "I can't find any more silver," she said.

Deke didn't respond.

She rolled her eyes, laughed at herself, and started to leave, changed her mind. "I mean,

God, Deke, look at me, huh? I am a college grad-
uate, for God's sake. I went to nursing school. I
have a goddamn master's degree in biology. I
stick needles in people's hairy asses, fix kids'
busted arms, and I . . . and I am a grown woman,
Deke, so what the hell am I doing?"

Polly stirred but didn't waken.

"Beats the shit outta me," he answered. "But
whatever it is, when you're done, would you
mind pulling the shades?"

"What? Why?"

"'Cause I don't want to see the moon."


Proctor said to Taz, "Do me a favor and put the
bags in the car."

He said to Vivian, "Do me a big favor. I need to
be alone for a minute."

And when he was, he returned to the window
and watched the moonlight take the color from
everything it touched. Hands in his pockets, he
tilted his head until it rested against the pane,
closed his eyes, and walked through each day
from the moment he'd arrived in Georgia. Step
by step; that's what he had done. Everything had
been step by step. Reacting instead of thinking.
No excuse that there hadn't been time. There had
been, but he hadn't taken it. He had not stepped
back and scanned the field, searching for the con-
nections which he now knew were all there. Step
by step. Point to point.

All these years, all that experience, and he hadn't bothered to draw on it, to even consider it.

A woman was dead because of him.

With no alternate universe to slip into and observe, he had no idea if Riza Noscu would still be alive if he had only taken the time.

It didn't matter.

Here, in this world, she was dead.

Son of a bitch, Proctor, she's dead.

He raised a fist and pushed it against the glass, pushed harder, and turned slowly when he felt Vivian in the room. She stood by the connecting door, without apology for the intrusion.

"Are you through?" she asked. "Beating yourself up, I mean. Are you done yet?"

His anger didn't last long.

"For the time being," he answered. "Yeah."

"Good."

"Later maybe."

"Not while I'm around."

No, he thought; you're probably right about that.

"What next?"

He crossed to the desk. "I'm going to see if I can kill two birds with one stone." He checked the telephone for instructions to connect to an outside line, and picked up the receiver. "Do you happen to know the number of the local police?"

\* \* \*

Mayor Posten stood to one side of his office window, portable telephone in one hand. He could see straight down to the steps, and up Alton Road, both of which were crowded with people. So far, he'd been lucky—they hadn't spotted him yet.

"Sweet Christ, Art, there are hundreds of them out there. Don't they need a permit or something?"

"You want to tell them that?"

Chanting, singing, some idiot with a battery-keyboard playing hymns. Placards and flags.

"Damnit, Art, they've even got those stupid torches lit. I feel like the peasants are about to burn the damn castle down."

"I told you to leave hours ago."

"I can't let them drive me away. That'd be flat wrong, and you know it."

Cheers and more hymns.

"If they break in, Richard, there isn't going to be a whole lot I can do. I'm outnumbered and outgunned. You'd just better pray that Reverend Carlton can control them."

"Pray? What the hell you think I've been doing for the past six hours, playing with myself? Look, send me a couple of boys who can sneak me out the back. This mob isn't going to last much longer. They'll wear themselves out by midnight."

"I'll do what I can, Mr. Mayor."

"I'm sure you will, Chief."

Posten hung up and returned to the window. He had long since taken off his white suit jacket to make himself less visible, and with no lights on inside he was pretty sure he was safe.

"You fools," he said quietly as he scanned the faces below. "Go home. Protect your little ones. Go home. Go home."

Then he looked up at the sky, saw the moon, and said, "Please. Please, not tonight."


When the connection was made, Proctor asked to speak to Officer Bobby Grace, if he was on duty.

"Mister," he was told, "in case you've been living on Mars or something, we got a little problem down here. I don't know where Bobby is, and I haven't got time to chase him down. If you want to leave a message, I can give it to him, but I'm not promising when he'll get it."

"I see. Well, maybe you could—"

"Wait. Hold it. There he is. Hang on a minute."

He was put on hold, so he picked up one of Madam Noscu's bullets and rolled it back and forth between his thumb and fingertips. Thinking nothing. Glancing over at Vivian, whose expression told him she knew precisely what he was doing and she didn't approve.

He looked away.

He didn't care.

"What?" a man's voice said sharply in his ear.

"Bobby Grace?"

"Who's asking?"

Proctor smiled. "This is Proctor. The man from up North?"

"Who? Oh. Yeah. So what do you want?"

"Well, I'm leaving town tonight—"

"What are you talking about? The airport's closed."

"Not for me it isn't."

Grace said nothing.

"So I'm leaving in a little while—I'm just about ready to head out to the airport—and before I left I wanted to ask you a question."

"Proctor, I ain't got time for—"

"Shut up, Grace."

Nothing on the line, then, but the station's noise, until, "What do you want?"

"Oh, that's easy. I'm probably going to make a stop in Atlanta on my way, to see some law-enforcement people I know. So tell me, Officer: Why the hell did you shoot Riza Noscu?"

# TWENTY

Taz had tested the car and assured Proctor it would be all right, for the couple of miles to the airport, anyway. And as long as they didn't meet a cop along the way. Then he wanted to know if they were really leaving tonight.

"As soon as the plane gets here."

"I still don't get it."

Before Proctor could answer, Vivian told him about the call, her tone carefully neutral.

"Holy shit," Taz said.

Proctor started the engine, switched on the headlamps, and listened for a few seconds to be sure Taz was right, that the car wouldn't die halfway to their destination.

"Are you sure it's him?" Vivian asked, looking straight ahead.

"Yes."

"What about Kranz? How can you be sure it's not him?"

*do you know what it's like to be crazy?*

"Because I don't think he's that good an actor." A glance over his shoulder. "Taz, when you looked for Kranz, did you happen to notice if there were any dumpsters back there?"

"Yep. A couple." And added, "Oh, hell."

Proctor drove around the end of the building to the back lot, pulled up beside two closed dumpsters huddled under a bare white bulb, and said, "Check."

The first was nearly empty, the second nearly full. Taz wasted no time being careful—he yanked plastic bags out and tossed them to the ground. When the level fell far enough, he climbed in, threw out more bags, then disappeared for a moment. When he reappeared, he climbed out, brushed himself off, and returned to the car.

Vivian said, "Well?"

Taz nodded somberly. "Was buried near the bottom so nobody would see him. I can't tell how it happened. A broken neck, I think, but I really can't tell for sure." As the car pulled away, he added, "Poor old guy."

Proctor drove as fast as he dared. There was no other traffic on the road, the moon so bright he almost didn't need the lights that bleached the blacktop a hard grey. The engine coughed once, and the car bucked, but it didn't stop. A warning light began to blink on the dashboard, a faint buzzing behind it.

When they pulled into the airport's deserted parking lot, he said, "If there's no one inside, we'll have to break in."

"I know we're going home and all," Taz said as they grabbed their bags and climbed out, "but why here?"

"Space," Proctor answered. "It's as close to home ground as we're going to get."

The doors were locked, but midway up he could see a maintenance man leaning on a floor polisher, taking a break. Proctor pounded, and the man looked his way, shook his head and shooed them with one hand.

Proctor pounded again, not stopping until the man, disgust in his posture, came to the door and yelled, "You blind, pal? We're closed."

Proctor pointed at the push-bar. "Open it."

The man turned away with a shake of his head, turned back when he heard a tapping, and saw Proctor's gun. This time there was no argument. Using a key from a ring on his belt, he unlocked the door and stepped hastily back as they walked in.

"Look, mister," he said, hands up, "I don't want any trouble, okay? I'm just the—"

Proctor looked at him. "Go away. Leave the building, and go away."

The man did, not looking back once.

Proctor pointed at the floor polisher. "Get rid of that, Taz, get it out of the way. And see if you can find the light switches. If you do, see if you can turn them all off but the ones down here." He pointed at the other end. "We'll be up there."

He moved in that direction, aware that Vivian had stayed behind with Taz. That was all right. He wanted this time, and he used it, noting the counter on his left and its divisions into the concessions—a fleeting hope that the rental girl wouldn't get in too much trouble—and the barely adequate security lights that burned above each one. On the right the glass wall, and the moon-touched runway.

When he reached the row of plastic seats, counting a dozen in all, he put his bag on one and tested the runway door to be sure it was locked.

Then he took out his gun and turned around to face the entrance.

He placed Vivian behind the seats, Taz behind the counter, both of them some ten feet closer to the entrance than he was. The darkness here was by no means complete, but he hoped Grace would be concentrating on him, which would give the others a chance to move if they had to without being noticed.

Taz propped his elbows on the counter ledge. "You're sure it's him."

Proctor nodded.

Taz frowned, trying to work it out. "Okay, but

aren't you supposed to be bitten or something first?"

Proctor looked at him. "That's the usual way, yes."

"So who bit him? I mean, doesn't that mean there's more than one of them out there?"

A thin cloud dimmed the moon. The terminal darkened briefly. Taz looked up sharply, waiting. When the moonlight brightened again, he blew out a breath, smiled weakly.

"Well?"

"I don't think so," Proctor answered, and immediately held up a hand. "Don't ask. I don't know. I just don't think so."

Taz shrugged. "Okay, but if you ask me, I think the son of a bitch likes it."

Proctor said nothing.

"What if it isn't him?" Vivian asked, seated and facing the runway. "What if you're wrong and it's someone else?"

He didn't answer.

Her voice whispered like the wind: "If you're wrong, Proctor, it's murder."

He didn't answer.

Bobby Grace had killed Riza because she knew what he was; he killed Kranz because the teacher had seen him transformed and, probably, had seen some or all of the transformation and could identify him. He had done both while he was human because he was arrogant enough to believe he could get away with it, and they were easier to get to during the daylight hours. He had no doubt that either the desk clerk or the motel manager had told Grace about Kranz being in the room. Why, he wasn't sure. Speculation would come later, after all the blood had dried.

And Taz was right—it was evident that Grace, cursed to be a shape-shifter, actually liked being a monster.

For him it wasn't a curse, it was an unholy blessing.

"Somebody's coming," Taz whispered.

Proctor watched the white cruiser coast up to the doors.

The damnable part of it was, Maudie Batts, the reason he was down here in the first place, was still missing, and he hadn't a clue where she had gone. If she was still alive.

Grace slid out of the car and put his hat on the roof.

Vivian said one more time, "What if you're wrong?"

Grace opened the door and stepped through, hitched up his belt and said cheerfully, "That you, Mr. North Man?"

As the door closed, a cold wind slipped in behind him. A late autumn wind that made Proctor's shoulders hunch, that made his skin tighten.

"Mr. North Man?"

Proctor didn't answer. If he was wrong, Grace

would use his own gun, and Proctor had to believe that neither Vivian nor Taz would miss; if he was right . . . two bullets each, that's all.

Two bullets each.

Grace bowed his head, shook it regretfully. "Now you know I can't let you talk to anyone, right? You do know that, don't you?"

Voice hollow in the empty terminal.

"And if you think I don't know you have help up there, you're dumber than I thought." He laughed. "So I guess I'll just have to even the odds."

When it happened, there was no dramatic sound of stretching bone or ripping flesh; when it happened, there was no cry of agony or a begging to be released; when it happened . . . there was a high loud laugh that rumbled swiftly into a snarl . . . there was a shimmer, a distortion, a rippling shadow in the air.

When it happened, there was a wolf larger than any other, whose slanted eyes were pale grey, whose pelt was the russet of a fox whose paws were black instead of white, whose tail was a whip, not a brush. The ears were up; the fangs were bared.

Claws ticking softly on the floor.

The tail switching back and forth, lazily.

Outside, the wind buffeted the building, making the glass walls shimmer, slipping drafts inside that sought to kill the warmth.

Proctor took a step forward. He couldn't see the others, but he could hear them shifting, and suddenly he hoped that if there was a crossfire they wouldn't shoot each other instead of Bobby Grace. He had enough on his conscience today; he didn't need that as well.

The wolf lifted its great head and howled, a deafening challenging howl that made Proctor grimace and look away, as if that would stop the needle-like pain that erupted briefly in his ears.

When he looked back, the wolf had stopped, and they stared at each other. For one nightmarish moment, when the creature moved its jaw, he thought it would speak. Instead, it growled. A deep-throated rumbling, long and steady, loud enough to fill the shadows.

Proctor adjusted his grip.

The cold made him think of dead leaves and mist and something flying across the face of the moon.

The growling stopped.

Proctor braced himself.

And it charged.

Proctor dropped to one knee and fired, but he was too late. The wolf had leapt almost sideways onto the counter and raced along the top, snarling as it pulled its lips back to expose its fangs. Suddenly Taz popped up, and in one brief action Proctor understood only in retrospect, the wolf snapped and clawed at Taz as it passed, and Taz, yelling and falling backward, fired twice into the ceiling.

On the floor again and running, and Proctor threw himself to one side, pulling his arms in tight to keep the wolf from reaching him as it passed, and skidded into a circle that slid him farther away.

Proctor aimed.

The wolf recovered its spin and lowered its head, but not its eyes.

Growling again, always growling.

Claws on the floor, ticking slowly, like a dying clock.

The wind rising to a muffled howl as a cloud coasted over the moon. Light and dark; dark and light.

When the wolf charged a second time, Proctor stood his ground, held his breath, pulled the trigger, cursed silently when he saw the gouge rip out of the floor underneath the creature's stomach. Again he threw himself to one side, but was unable to get to his feet and slid hard into the chairs, whacking his head and shoulder on a metal leg.

Dazed, he tried to stand, and dazed he said nothing when Vivian shoved him back down with one hand and stood in front of him.

She fired once, and the wolf screamed and lost

its footing, landed on its side and slid, legs kicking frantically, jaws snapping helpless at the hole in its chest.

Screamed, and howled, until she walked right up to it and put her second bullet in its head.

# TWENTY-ONE

The flight left long before dawn.

Proctor had given up trying to find ways to thank Vivian for what she had done, amused at her embarrassment, chastened by her act. So he strapped himself in and let himself drift into a doze where he could direct all his dreams, and where he was the hero who rode into town and saved all the people.

What he did not do was answer that question: what if you're wrong?

He did not have to.

She already knew the answer, and she would have to live with it, even though the situation hadn't happened. It wasn't that she hadn't seen his justice before; this would have been the first time she had seen it at his own hand

The plane shuddered. Just a little.

His eyes flickered open, and he saw her watching him.

A smile: "Don't," he said. "You'll just drive

yourself crazy." He shifted and closed his eyes
again. "It's done. Now we have another mystery
for Doc to work on, and I'm not giving odds that
he won't solve it."

"The globe?"

He nodded.

She pushed a hand back through her hair. "So
what do you think?"

"I'm not sure."

"Humor me."

He almost laughed. "Okay." He looked outside, at the dark still waiting for dawn. "I
think . . . I'm guessing it's what we found pieces
of in Kansas."

She shook her head. "That's no guess, Proctor,
and you know it."

"Yeah, I guess so." A quick grin at her pained
look before his expression grew somber. "Whatever it is, whatever it does, it belongs to them.
The ones who are trying to stop me. Us. From
doing whatever it is we're doing that's pissed
them off."

He knew she wanted to ask who "they" were,
but she also knew he didn't know the answer.

She looked away, looked back. "And Miriam
Tackett's daughter?"

A long while before he said, "If she came across
Grace, I don't think she made it. If she didn't . . .
we know enough that she was alive less than two
months ago."

"So . . . what do we tell her mother?"

The plane shuddered again.

"I don't know, Viv. I swear I don't know."

"Vivian," she said testily.

"Yeah," he said. "Right." One eye opened. "Are you going to let me sleep now?"

She grinned. "Maybe, Mr. Proctor."

But she said nothing more, and his doze became a sleep, and in his dream he saw Petra, who would not speak to him, and would not stay.

A touch on his arm.

He opened his eyes, saw her staring.

"What?"

"They're going to come after us, aren't they?"

No reassuring smile this time. "Yes. One way or another."

"It's connected, then. With Celeste and Maudie, and Ginger Hong."

The sun had finally risen.

He looked at the landscape, the hills and farm below, a river and a highway. He didn't have to answer, because she already knew, but just wanted him to say it. Say it aloud so it would be real.

Finally: "Yes."

A nod, and she turned away, folded her arms across her chest and closed her eyes.

He watched her for quite a while, not for the first time thinking what an amazing woman she was. Bodyguard, confidante, incredibly level-headed in situations that would drive other people into perpetual nightmares—

"Don't stare," she whispered without opening her eyes. "It's rude."

Caught, he looked out the window again with an apologetic grunt.

They'd be home in a few hours. He was grateful for the time. He'd need it to prepare himself for what he would tell the others—that from now on, nothing at Black Oak would ever be the same, no case ever again could be taken at face value.

Whoever, or whatever, had created that amber globe would be after him and his.

And he was almost certain, now, that Doc Falcon had been the first casualty in what might turn out to be a war.

In the restroom, Taz stood in front of the mirror with his shirt off, looking at a long scratch on his upper right arm, and a smaller red mark near his shoulder. He had wiped the blood away, but nothing that remained helped him.

He had said nothing about it to either Proctor or Vivian. He needed to know, first. He had to be sure.

It had happened so fast he barely remembered a thing except for those eyes and those teeth and the foul smell of its breath, the gunfire . . . and the screams.

Tomorrow, he thought; I'll tell them tomorrow.

But he had to know, first.

He had to know if he'd been bitten.

# Next, in *Black Oak*

In a cavernous room with very little light, there are voices, some touched with panic, other edged with anger:

"He has one, damnit. It's only a matter of time."

"Nonsense. He has no idea what it is. A bauble, nothing more."

"I don't give a damn if he thinks it's a bauble or part of the Crown Jewels. This time he has to die."

"Agreed. The question is—"

A third voice, quieter, more forceful:

"Enough. We will use the Three. See that it happens."

There is no more talk.

There is only a soft wind, and the sound of claws scraping against a stone floor.

In the desert that spreads across the Arizona-New Mexico border there is an excavation of a previously lost community whose descendants now live on a mesa northeast of Albuquerque. No one had ever believed the Konochine Indians had traveled this far west. No one knew why they would.

This is the third attempt to rescue the remaining buildings from the desert sands.

It isn't going very well.

Too many people are dying.

"I don't get it," says Ethan Proctor, standing at the back door. "He's never missed a day."

Lana Kelaleha, his office manager, is on the small back porch. "He says he picked up some kind of bug when you were in Georgia. He sounded awful."

"Lana, this is the fourth time in two weeks Taz has called in sick. I need him here, not feeling sorry for himself in bed."

"But—"

"Send Doc over to his place. Now. I want to know what's wrong." Proctor rubs the back of his neck slowly. "He isn't sick, Lana. I don't know what's wrong, but he isn't sick."

Proctor answers the doorbell late one afternoon, and sees a tall woman on the porch. She is slender, with short brown hair, large brown eyes, and a smile as false as any he has ever seen. Although he has never met her, he's pretty sure that he knows her, or knows of her.

It comes to him before she can introduce herself:

"Alicia Blaine," he says.

Her smile widens. "Very good, Mr. Proctor. Very good."

He steps aside and invites her in. "What can I do for you?"

"That's easy," she answers, trailing a finger along his jaw as she passes him. "I want to persuade you to forget about my sister. Stop looking for her. Stop tormenting my father."

Twenty minutes later:

"You're making a mistake, Proctor."

"Maybe. But Franklin couldn't change my mind, either."

"My brother is . . . not like me. And before we get into the nonsense about whether I'm threatening you or not . . . I am. Stay away, Proctor. Stay away from my father."

A body is found in the basement of a small museum in San Diego. It used to be a man. Now it is little more than bones and flesh.

It looks like a mummy.

It isn't.

# Investigate the odd with

(0-451)

☐ **VAMPIRE$** *John Steakley*                45153-8 / $6.50
It's a tough job killing vampires, but somebody's got to
do it. And Jack Crow and his dedicated vampire van-
quishers are those somebodies. They work hard, party
hard, and die hard. This is their story.

☐ **STORM FRONT** *Book One of the Dresden Files*

*Jim Butcher*                                 457811 / $6.99
Meet Harry Dresden, private detective, resident of Chicago,
wizard. He will find lost items, conduct paranormal investigations, and identify for you things that go bump in the
night....

☐ **FADED STEEL HEAT** *Glen Cook*          45479-0 / $6.99
Garrett is an investigator, living and working in a city
inhabited by all manners of being—Dwarves, Elves,
Humans, drop dead gorgeous redheads. With Garrett,
Cook has created one of the most fantastic hard-boiled
detectives ever.

---

# LOOK WHAT WE HAVE FOR YOU NEXT MONTH!